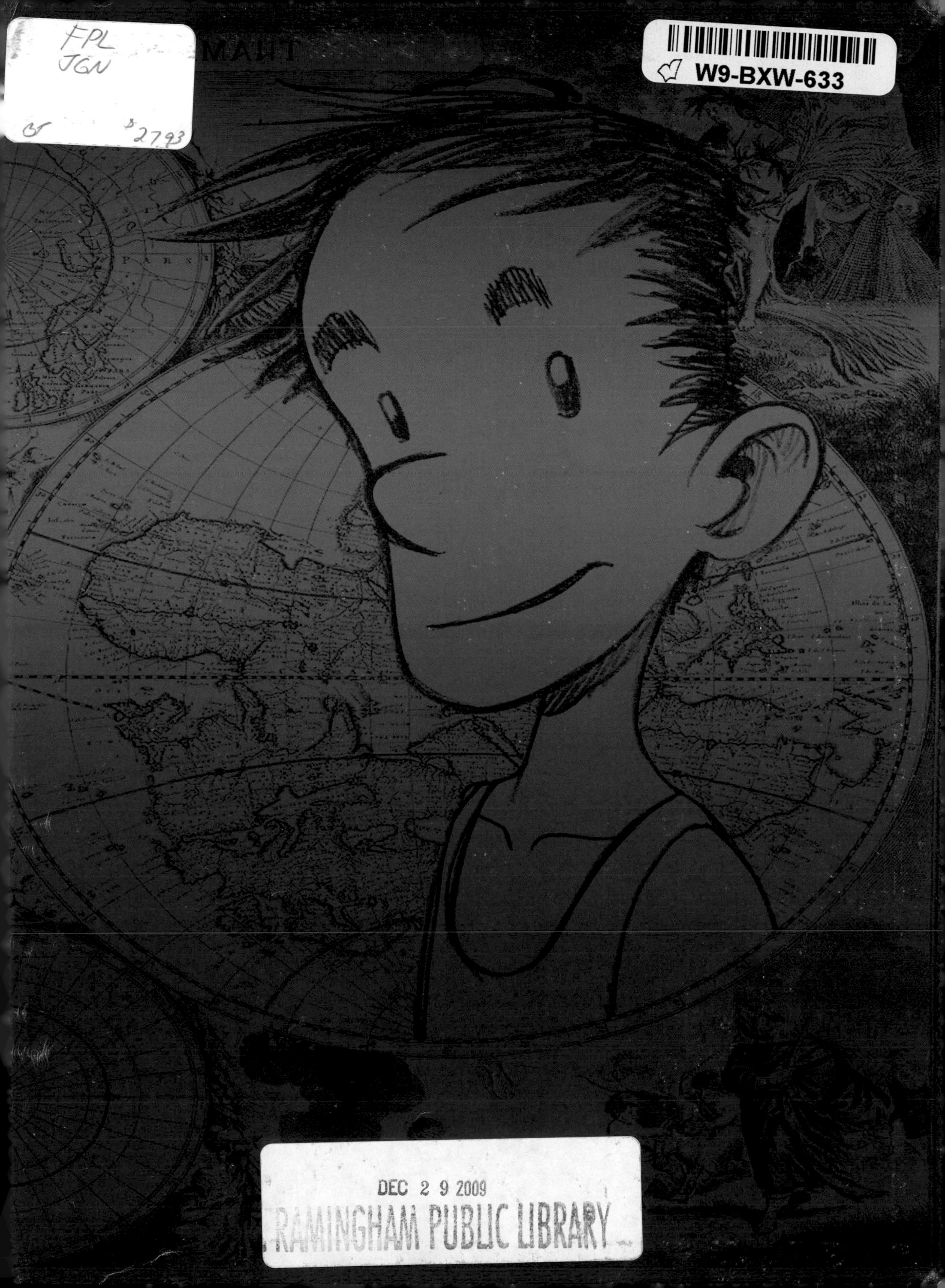

the ELSEWHERE CHRONICLES

BOOK TWO
THE SHADOW SPIES

ART
BANNISTER

STORY
NYKKO

COLORS
JAFFRÉ

GRAPHIC UNIVERSE™ • MINNEAPOLIS • NEW YORK

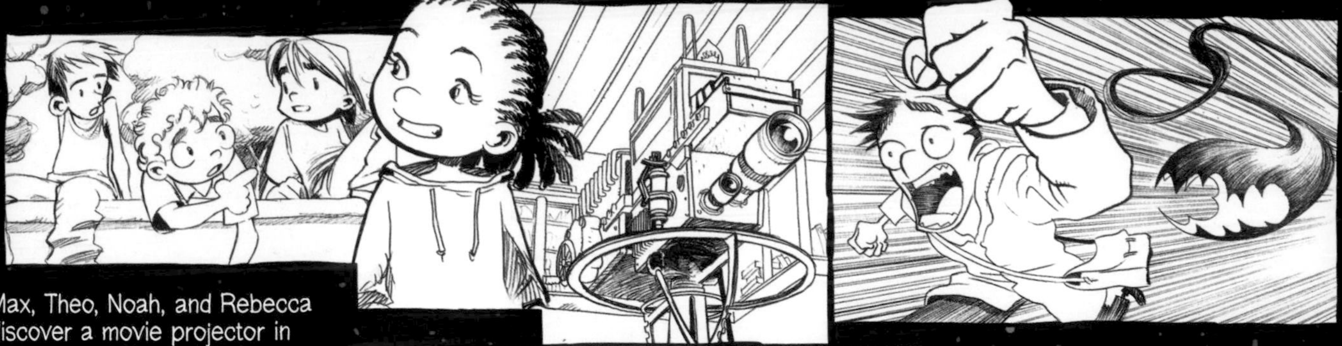

Max, Theo, Noah, and Rebecca discover a movie projector in the house of Rebecca's late Grandpa Gabe that opens a passageway into another world.

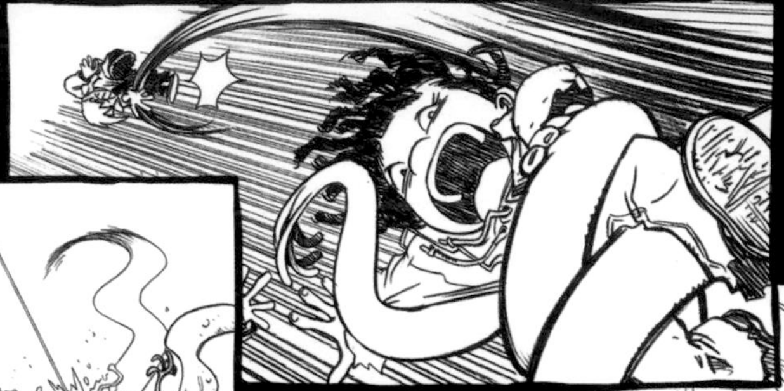

Unwisely, Rebecca turns on the projector. Grabbed by a tentacled monster, she is saved thanks to the help of brave Max and a mysterious warrior woman.

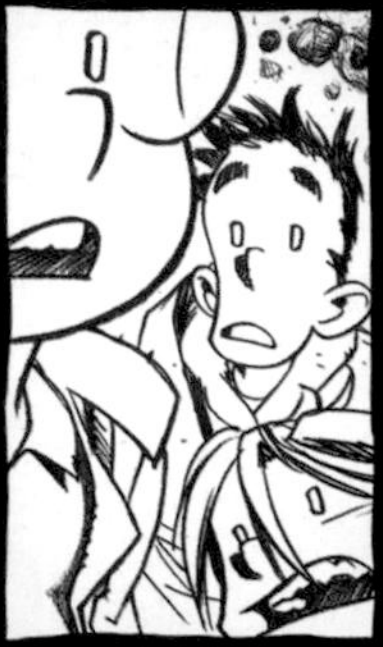

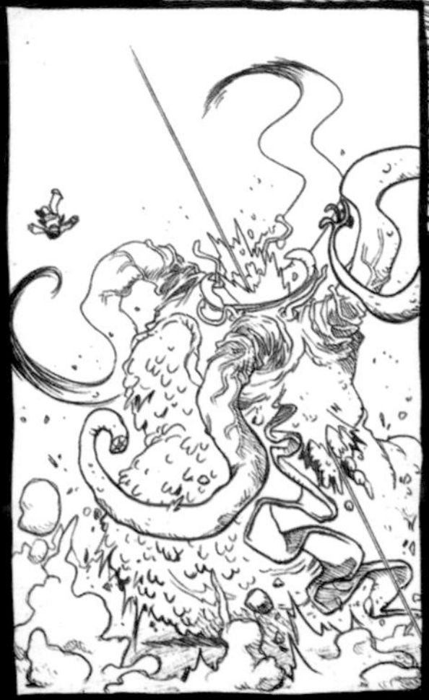

Now trapped in the other world, Max and Rebecca are counting on Theo and Noah to reopen the passageway. They don't know that the projector is broken.

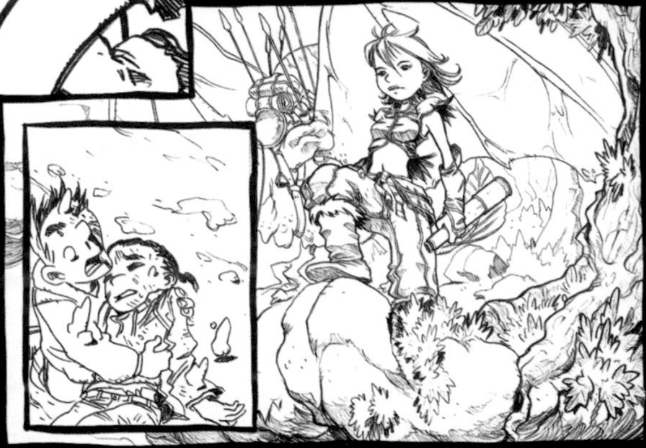

Thank you to my parents for their unfailing support.

Thank you to Denis and Laurence for their sensible editorial advice and the 24-hour hotline.

Thank you to my sweet Flora, without whom this book, at least the art, would be only a shadow of itself.

And next, thanks also to the other two guys, because they've done a great job too.

—Bannister

Norgavol, why did we have to leave so quickly?
I'd really love for you to tell me about my grandfather.
I understand, my dear girl. But the Master of Shadows must not discover your existence, or he will destroy your world as surely as he has destroyed ours.
If my people are too weak to battle him, it is at least our duty to keep the disease from spreading.

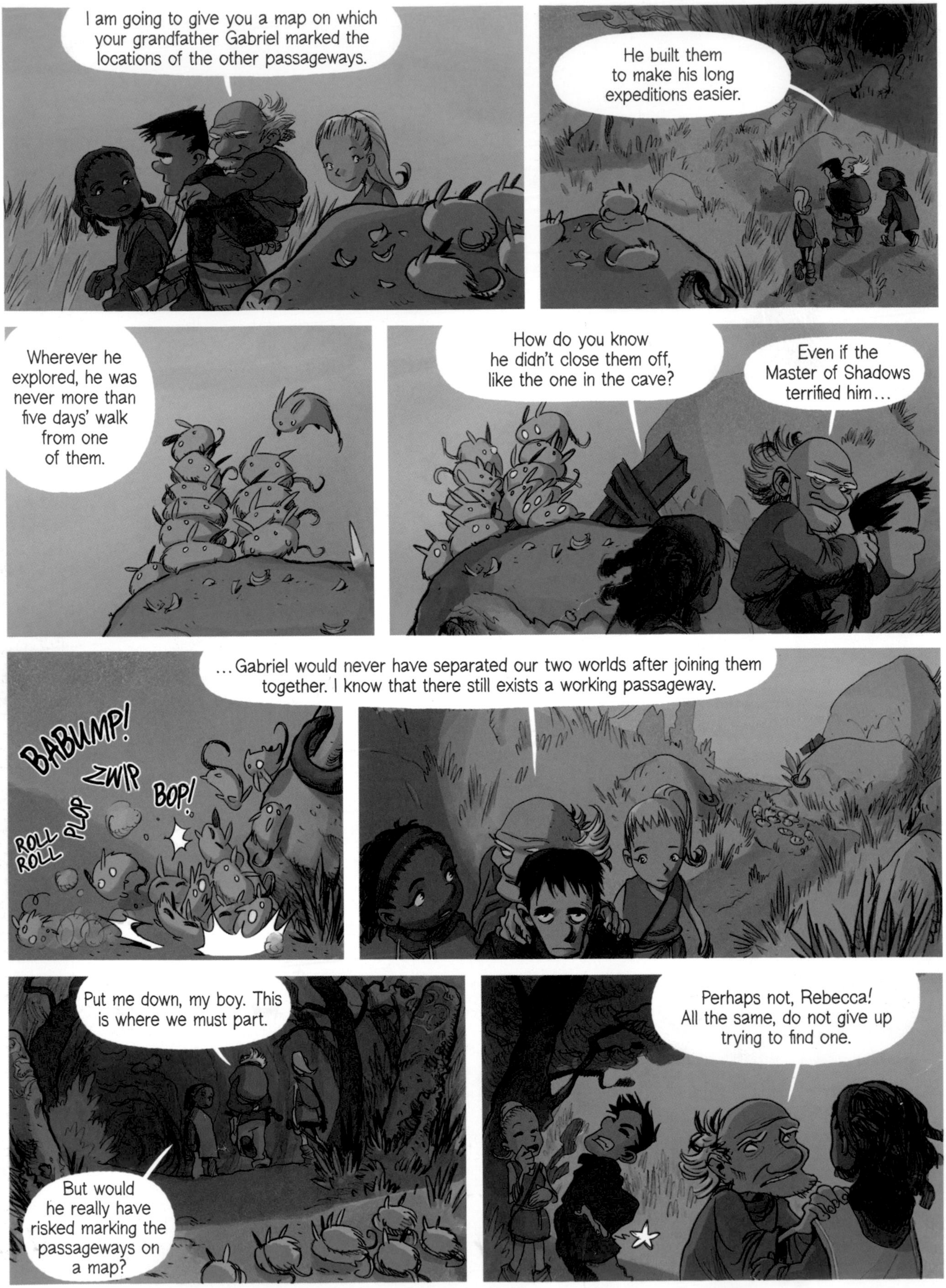
I am going to give you a map on which your grandfather Gabriel marked the locations of the other passageways.
He built them to make his long expeditions easier.
Wherever he explored, he was never more than five days' walk from one of them.
How do you know he didn't close them off, like the one in the cave?
Even if the Master of Shadows terrified him...
...Gabriel would never have separated our two worlds after joining them together. I know that there still exists a working passageway.
BABUMP!
ZWIP
BOP!
PLOP
ROLL ROLL
Put me down, my boy. This is where we must part.
But would he really have risked marking the passageways on a map?
Perhaps not, Rebecca! All the same, do not give up trying to find one.

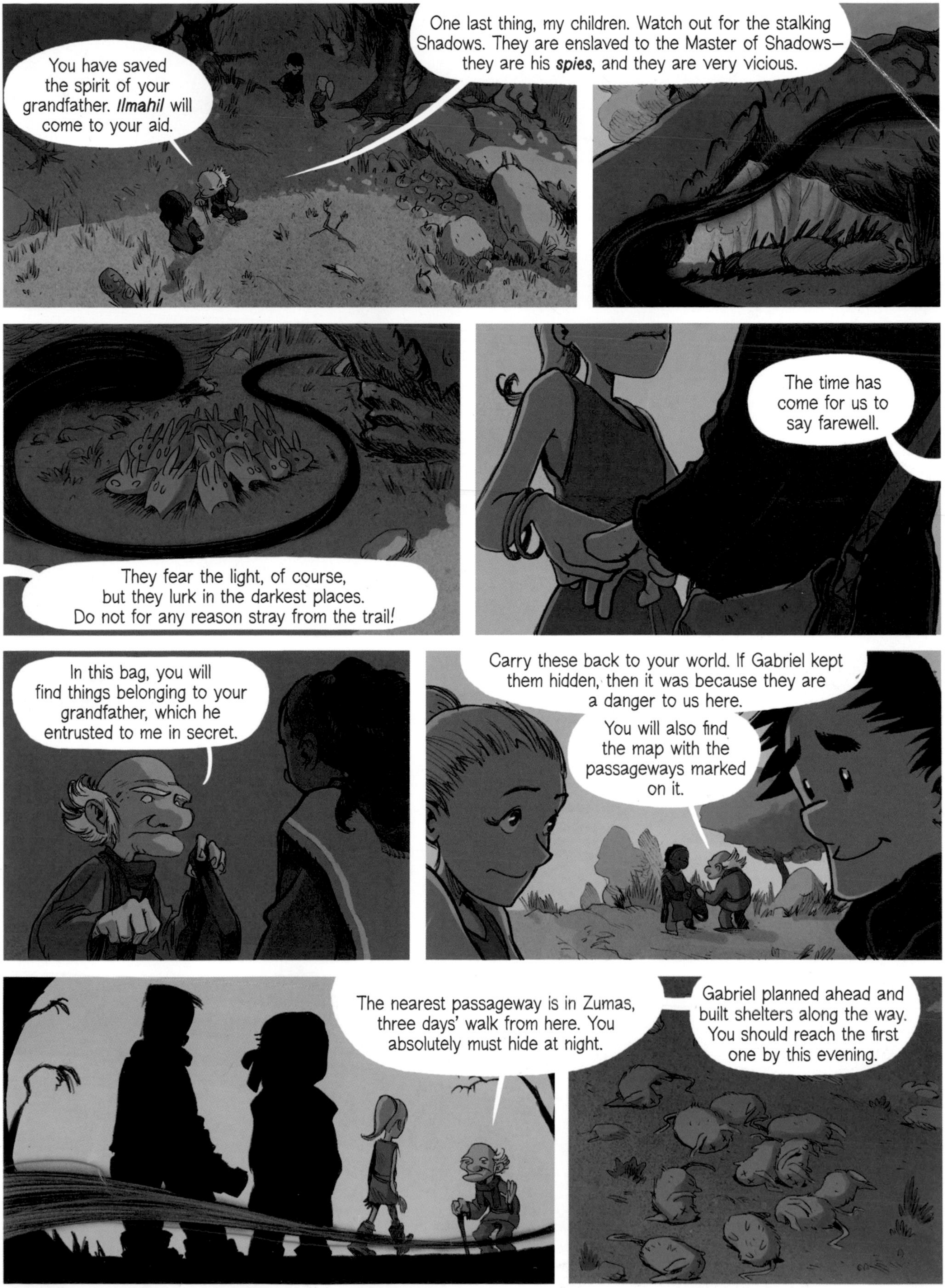
You have saved the spirit of your grandfather. *Ilmahil* will come to your aid.
One last thing, my children. Watch out for the stalking Shadows. They are enslaved to the Master of Shadows—they are his ***spies***, and they are very vicious.
They fear the light, of course, but they lurk in the darkest places. Do not for any reason stray from the trail!
The time has come for us to say farewell.
In this bag, you will find things belonging to your grandfather, which he entrusted to me in secret.
Carry these back to your world. If Gabriel kept them hidden, then it was because they are a danger to us here.
You will also find the map with the passageways marked on it.
The nearest passageway is in Zumas, three days' walk from here. You absolutely must hide at night.
Gabriel planned ahead and built shelters along the way. You should reach the first one by this evening.

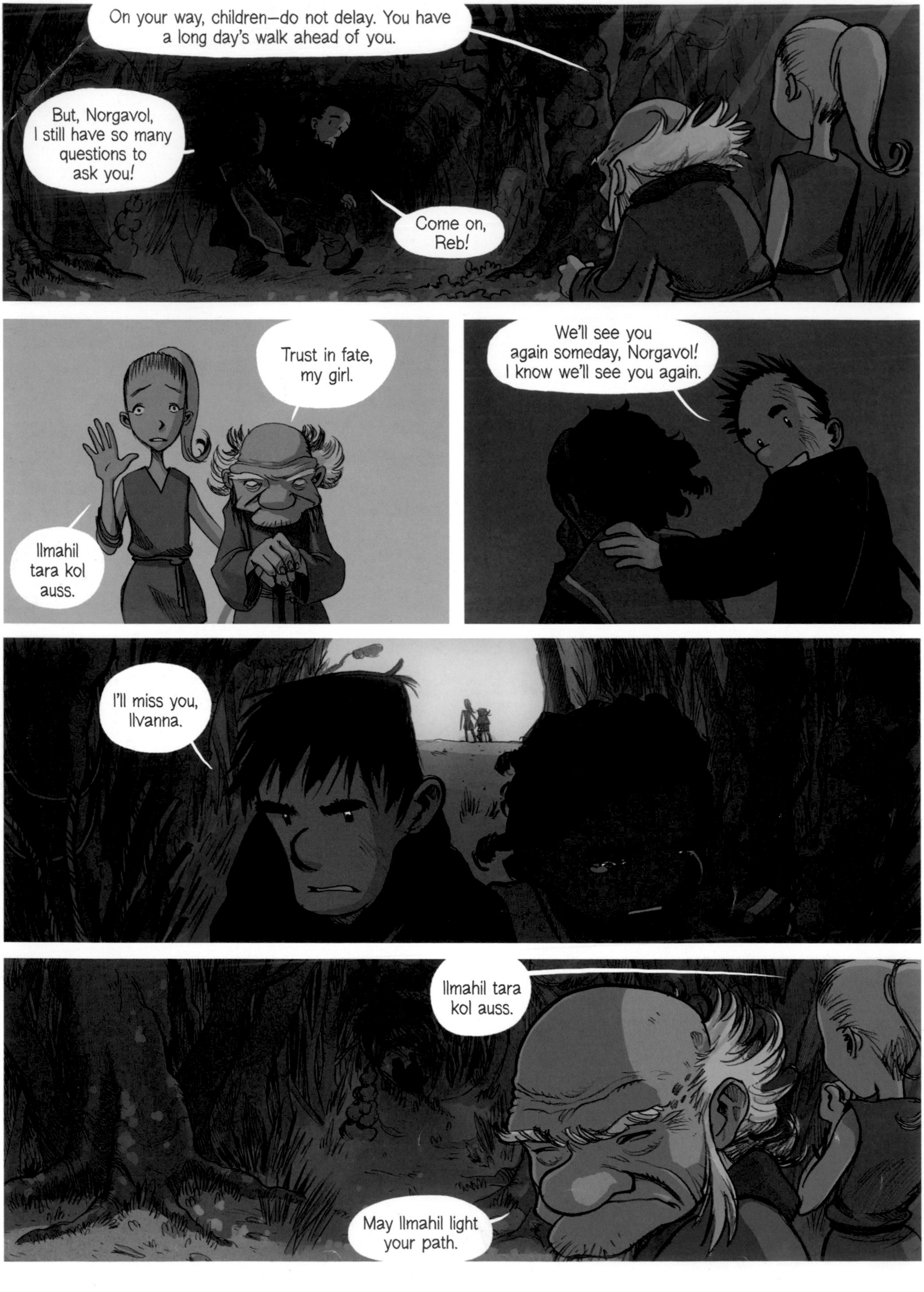
On your way, children—do not delay. You have a long day's walk ahead of you.
But, Norgavol, I still have so many questions to ask you!
Come on, Reb!
Trust in fate, my girl.
Ilmahil tara kol auss.
We'll see you again someday, Norgavol! I know we'll see you again.
I'll miss you, Ilvanna.
Ilmahil tara kol auss.
May Ilmahil light your path.

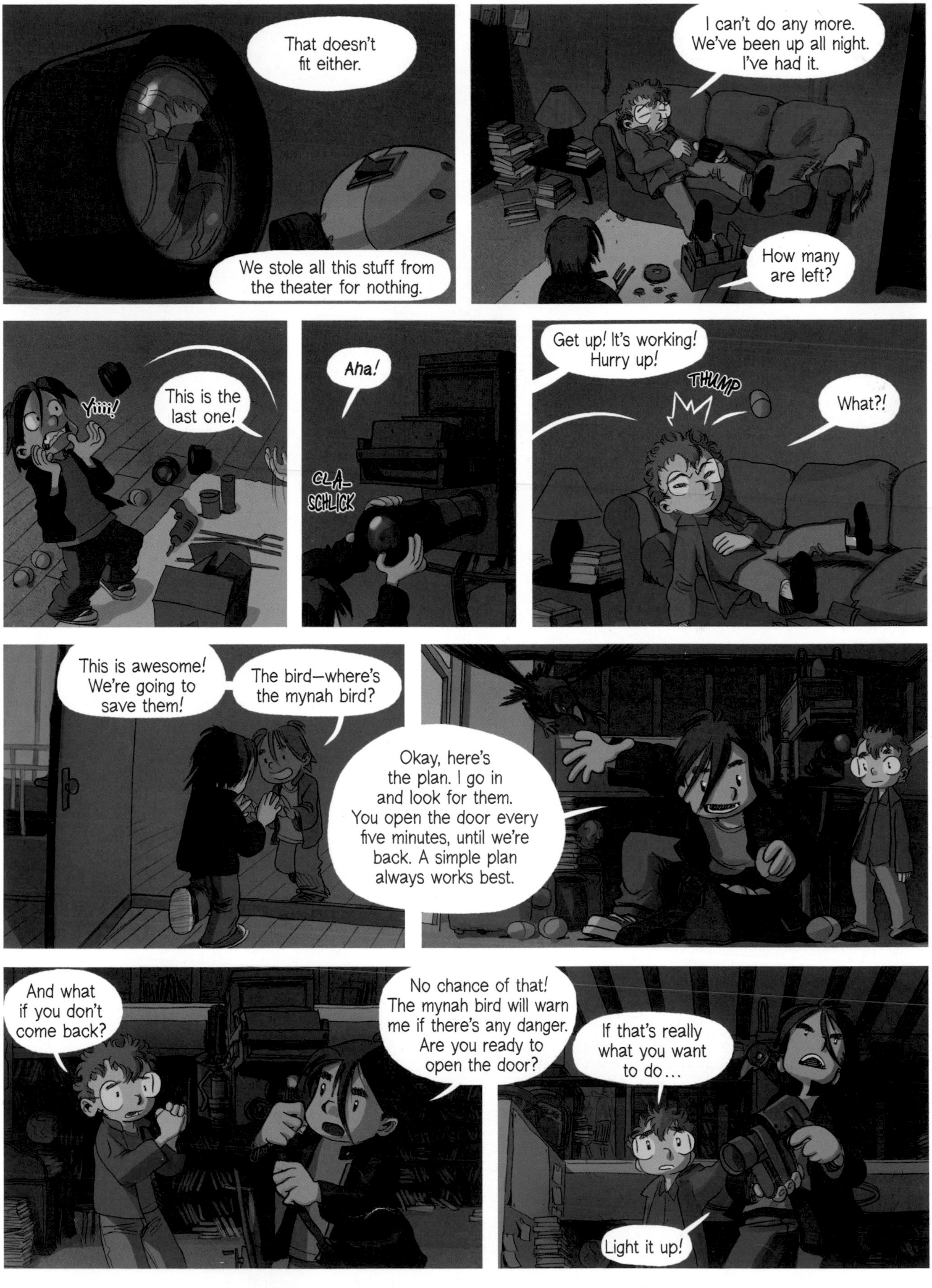
That doesn't fit either.
We stole all this stuff from the theater for nothing.
I can't do any more. We've been up all night. I've had it.
How many are left?
Yiiii!
This is the last one!
Aha!
CLA-SCHLICK
Get up! It's working! Hurry up!
THUMP
What?!
This is awesome! We're going to save them!
The bird—where's the mynah bird?
Okay, here's the plan. I go in and look for them. You open the door every five minutes, until we're back. A simple plan always works best.
And what if you don't come back?
No chance of that! The mynah bird will warn me if there's any danger. Are you ready to open the door?
If that's really what you want to do…
Light it up!

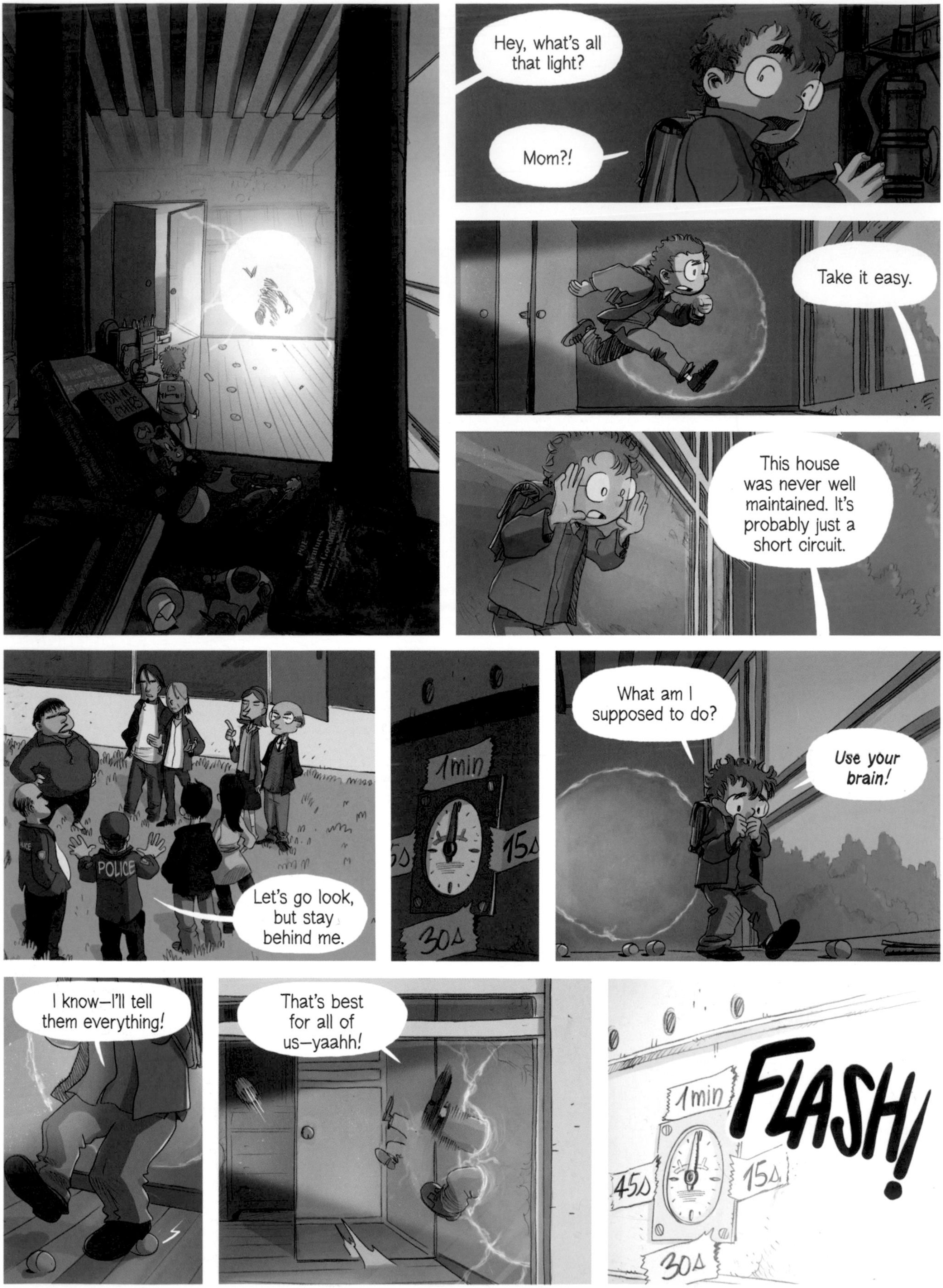
Hey, what's all that light?
Mom?!
Take it easy.
This house was never well maintained. It's probably just a short circuit.
Let's go look, but stay behind me.
1min
15s
30s
What am I supposed to do?
Use your brain!
I know—I'll tell them everything!
That's best for all of us—yaahh!
1min
45s
15s
30s
FLASH!

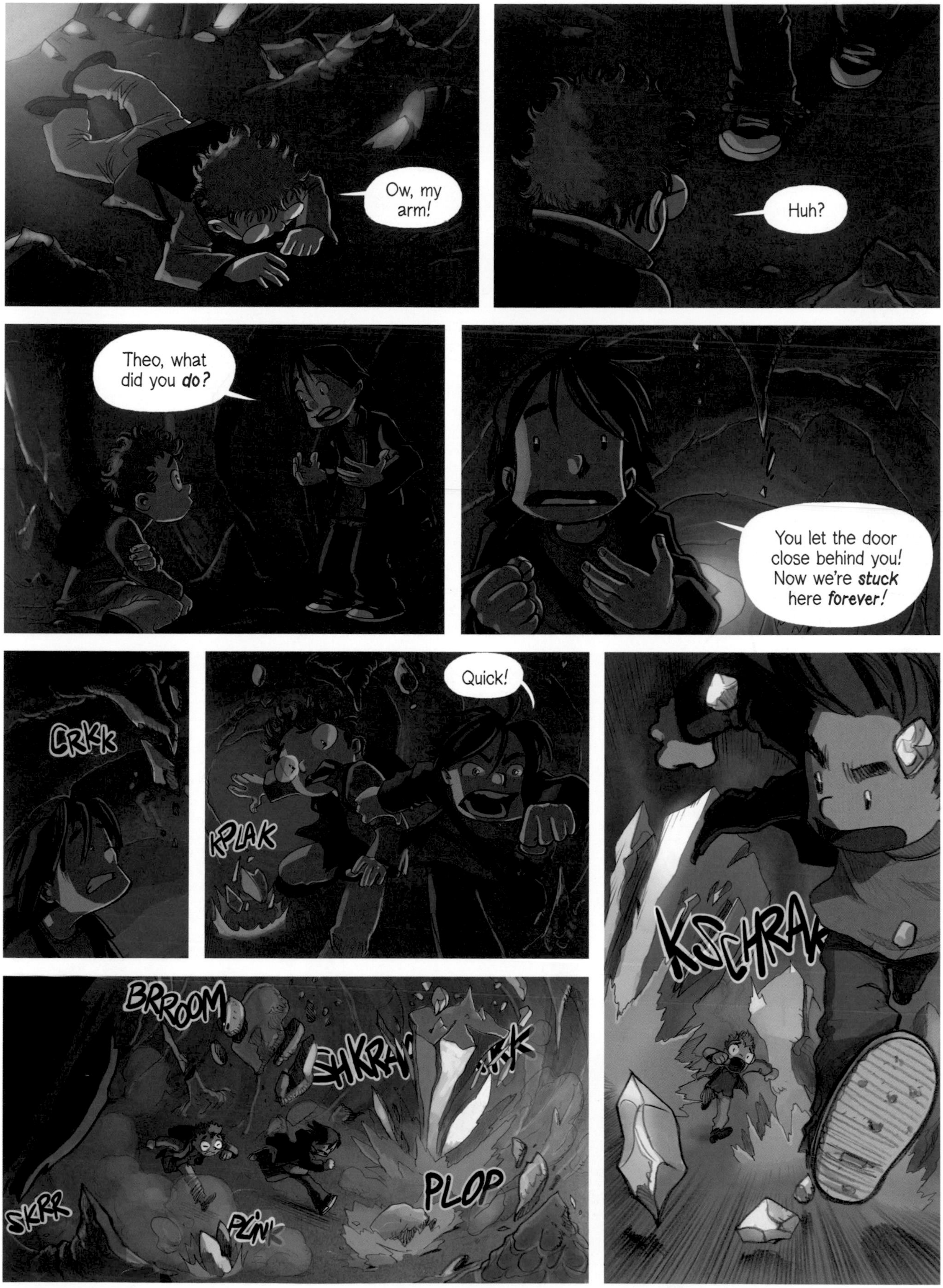
Ow, my arm!
Huh?
Theo, what did you do?
You let the door close behind you! Now we're stuck here forever!
CRKK
Quick!
KPLAK
KSCHRAK
BRROOM
SHKRAK
PLOP
SKRR
PLINK

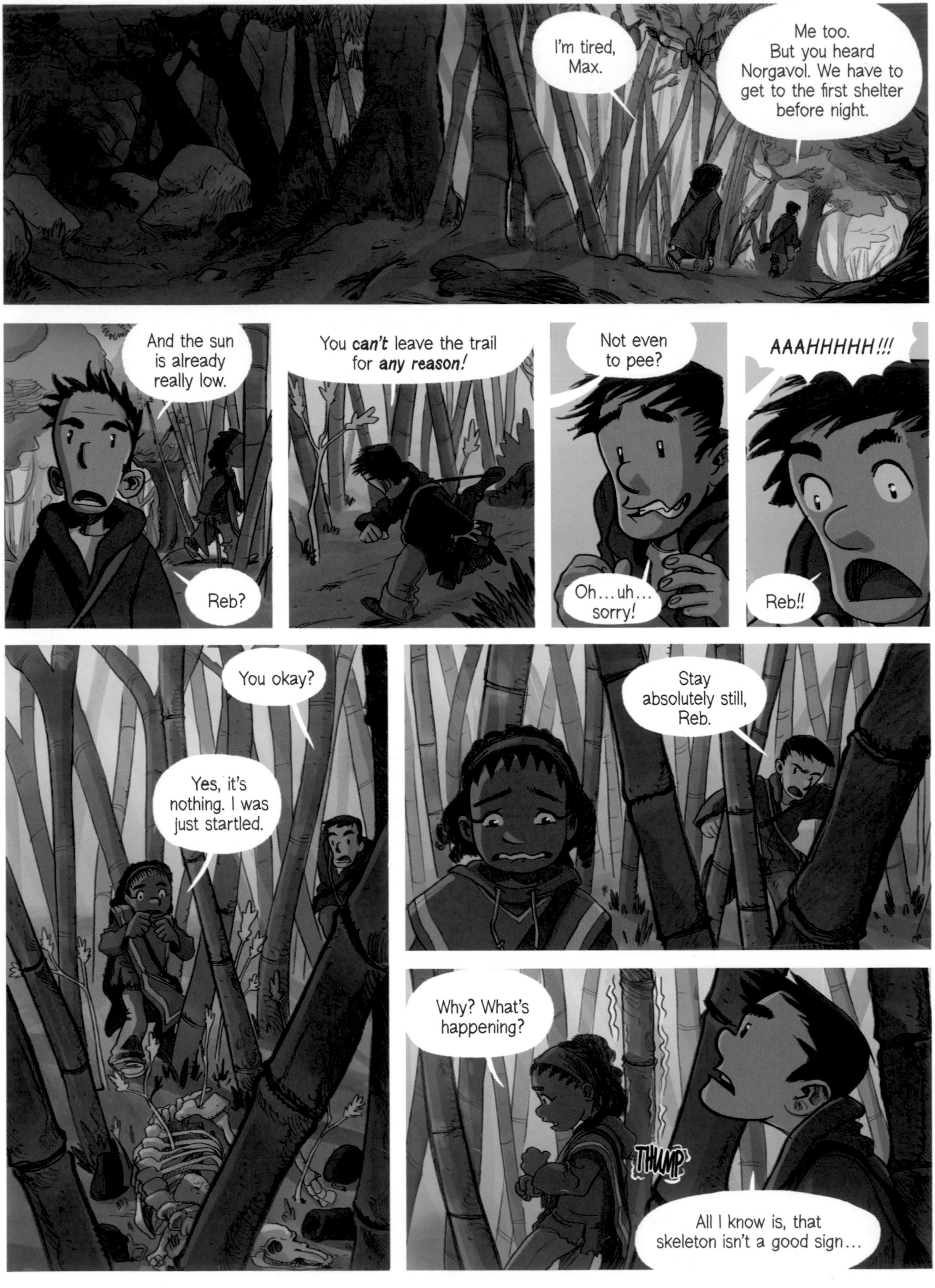
I'm tired, Max.
Me too. But you heard Norgavol. We have to get to the first shelter before night.
And the sun is already really low.
Reb?
You **can't** leave the trail for ***any reason!***
Not even to pee?
Oh...uh... sorry!
AAAHHHHH!!!
Reb!!
You okay?
Yes, it's nothing. I was just startled.
Stay absolutely still, Reb.
Why? What's happening?
THUMP
All I know is, that skeleton isn't a good sign...

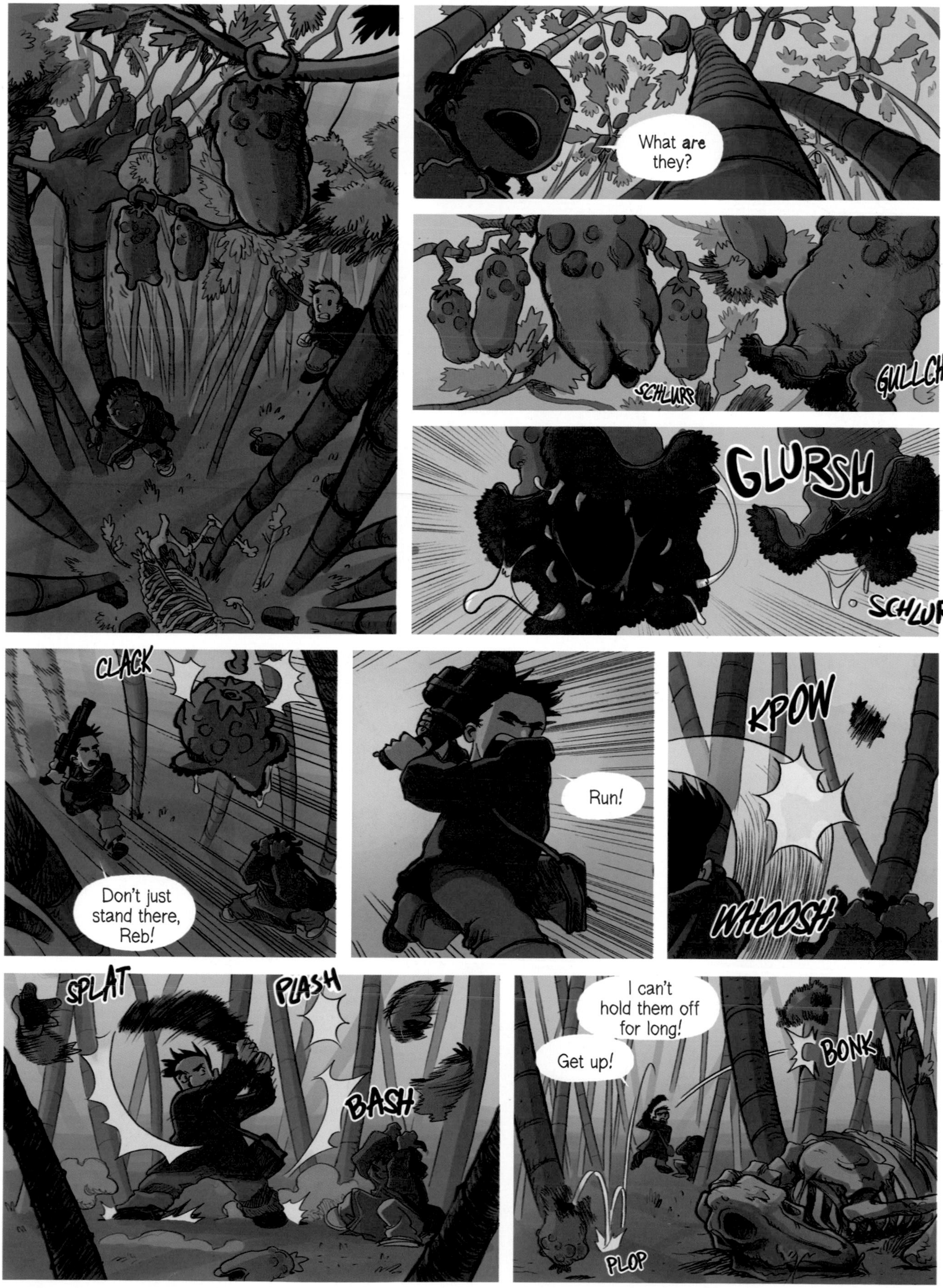
What are they?
SCHLURP
GULLCH
GLURSH
SCHLURP
CLACK
Don't just stand there, Reb!
Run!
KPOW
WHOOSH
SPLAT
PLASH
BASH
I can't hold them off for long!
Get up!
BONK
PLOP

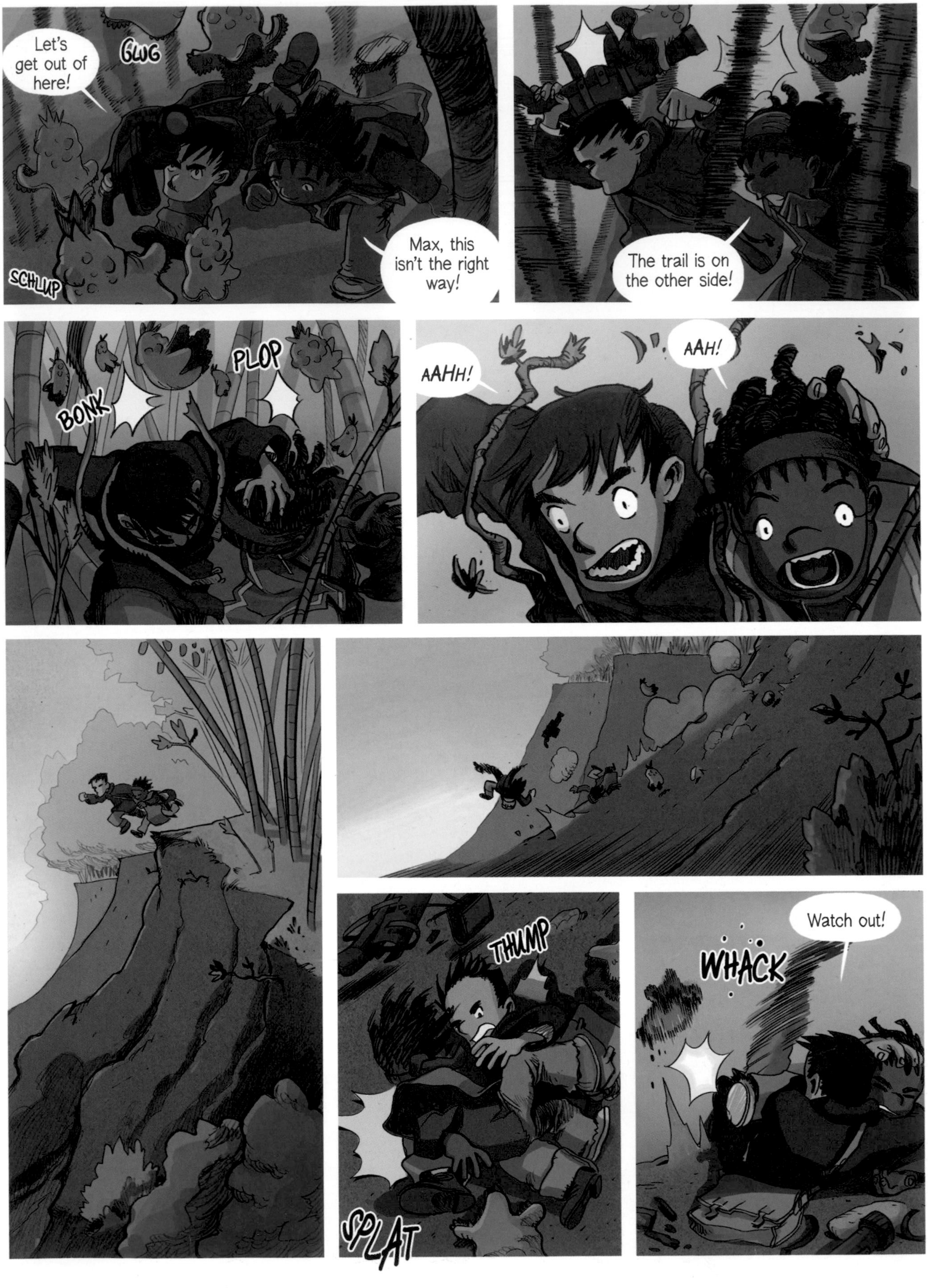
Let's get out of here!
GLUG
SCHLUP
Max, this isn't the right way!
The trail is on the other side!
BONK
PLOP
AAHH!
AAH!
THUMP
SPLAT
Watch out!
WHACK

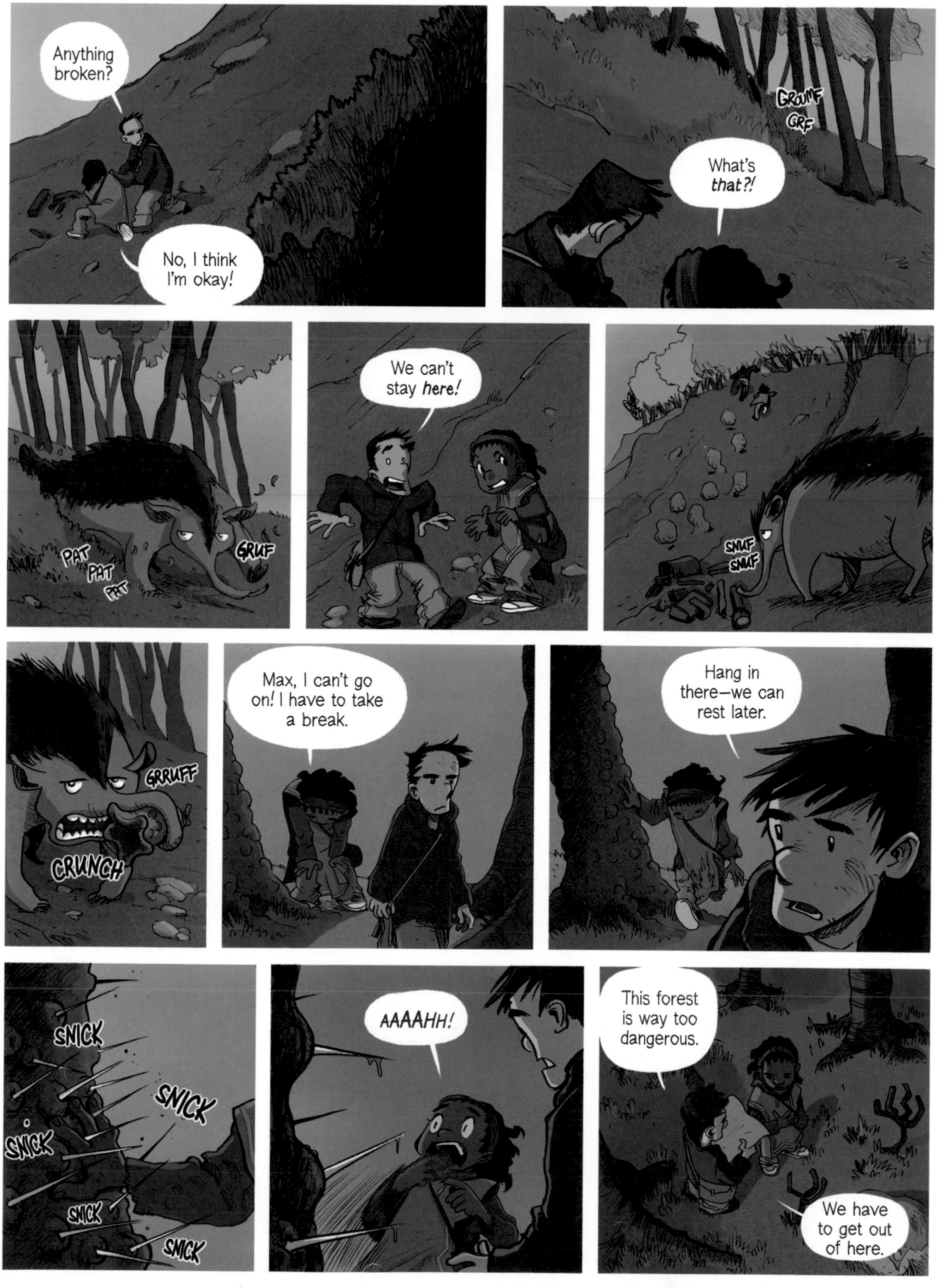
Anything broken?
No, I think I'm okay!
GROUMF
GRF
What's *that?!*
PAT
PAT
PAT
GRUF
We can't stay *here!*
SNUF
SNUF
GRRUFF
CRUNCH
Max, I can't go on! I have to take a break.
Hang in there—we can rest later.
SNICK
SNICK
SNICK
SNICK
SNICK
AAAAHH!
This forest is way too dangerous.
We have to get out of here.

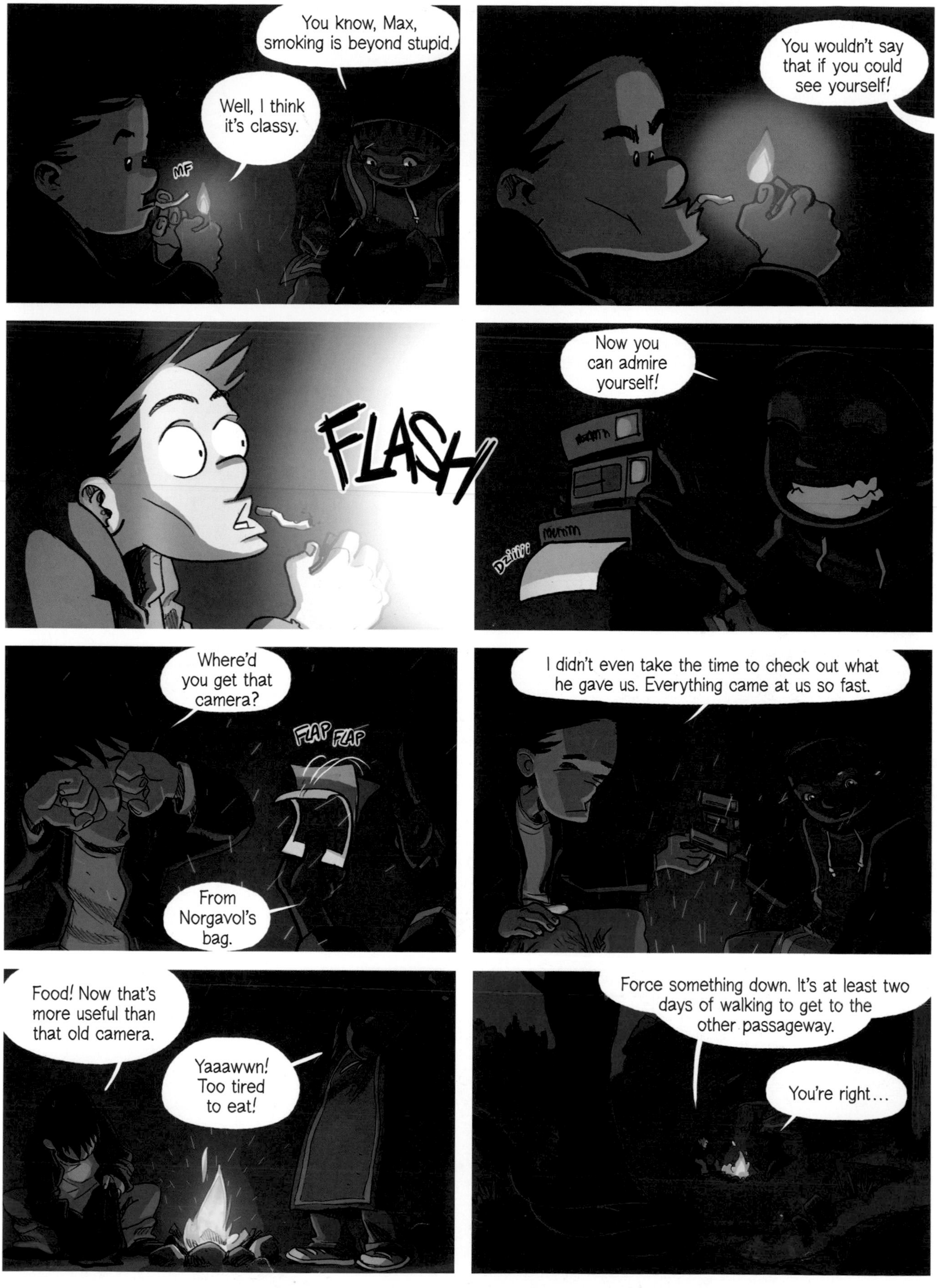
You know, Max, smoking is beyond stupid.
Well, I think it's classy.
MF
You wouldn't say that if you could see yourself!
FLASH
Now you can admire yourself!
Dziiiii
Where'd you get that camera?
FLAP FLAP
From Norgavol's bag.
I didn't even take the time to check out what he gave us. Everything came at us so fast.
Food! Now that's more useful than that old camera.
Yaaawwn! Too tired to eat!
Force something down. It's at least two days of walking to get to the other passageway.
You're right...

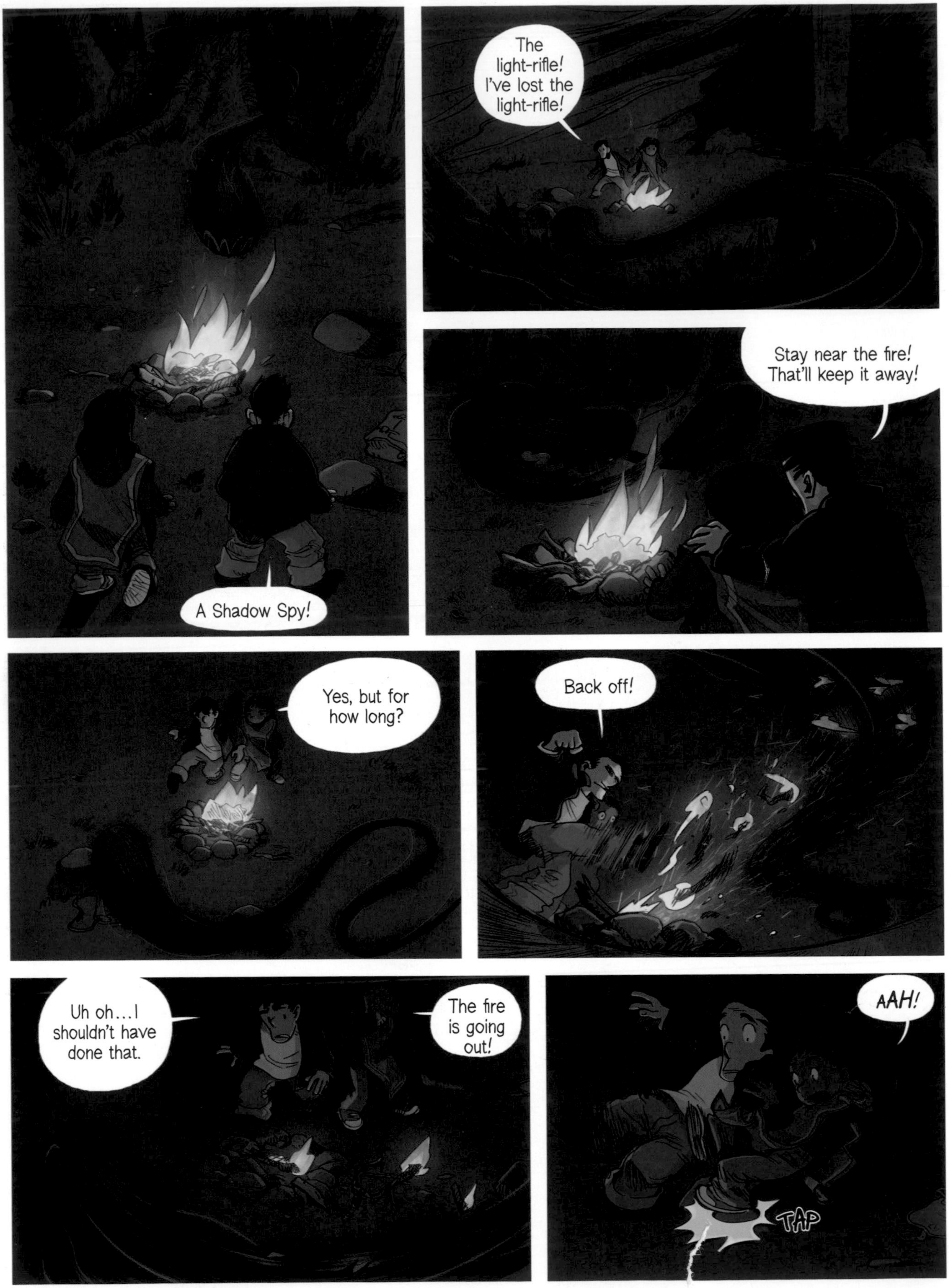
A Shadow Spy!
The light-rifle! I've lost the light-rifle!
Stay near the fire! That'll keep it away!
Yes, but for how long?
Back off!
Uh oh...I shouldn't have done that.
The fire is going out!
AAH!
TAP

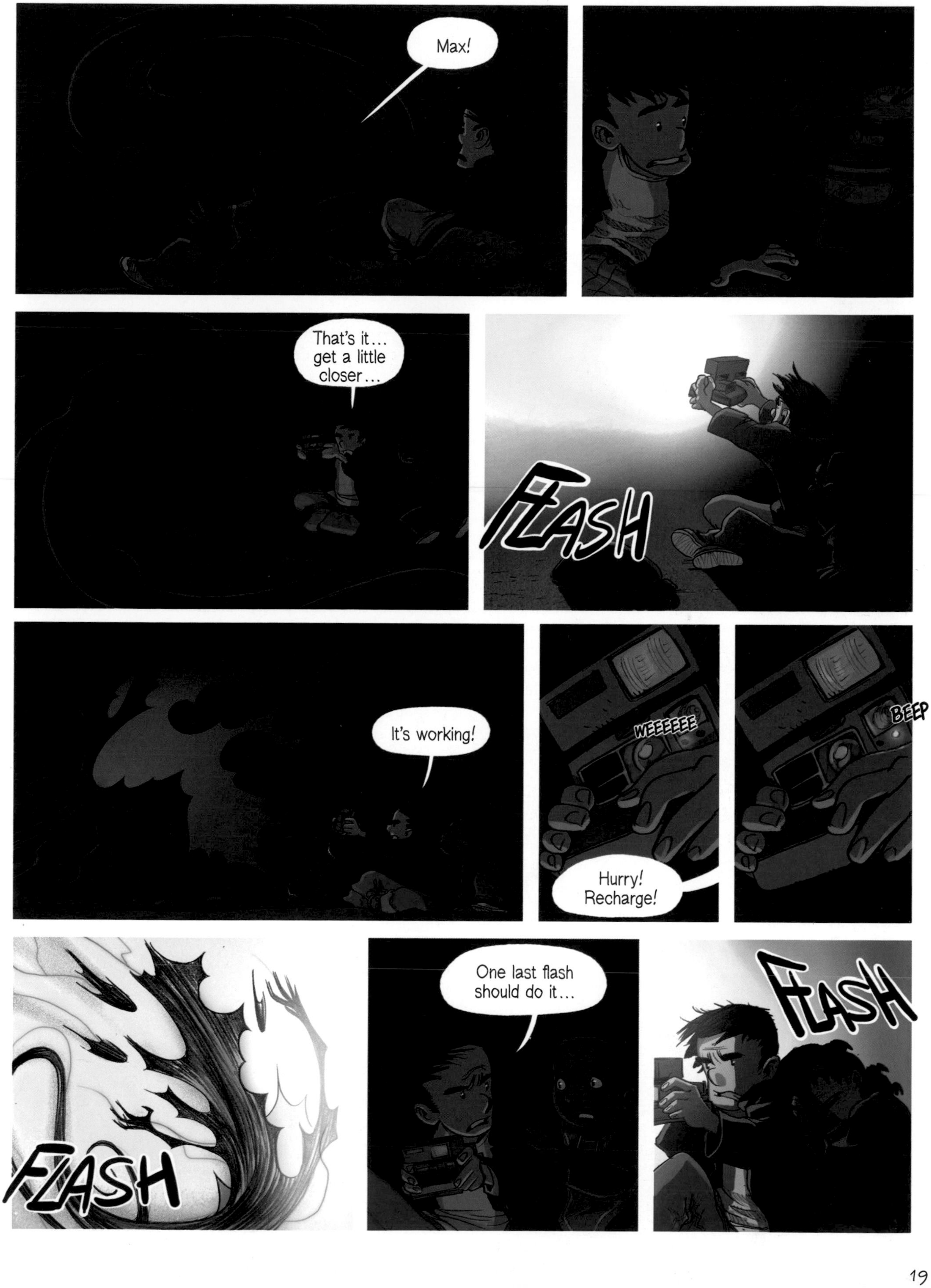

Max!
That's it... get a little closer...
FLASH
It's working!
WEEEEEE
Hurry! Recharge!
BEEP
FLASH
One last flash should do it...
FLASH

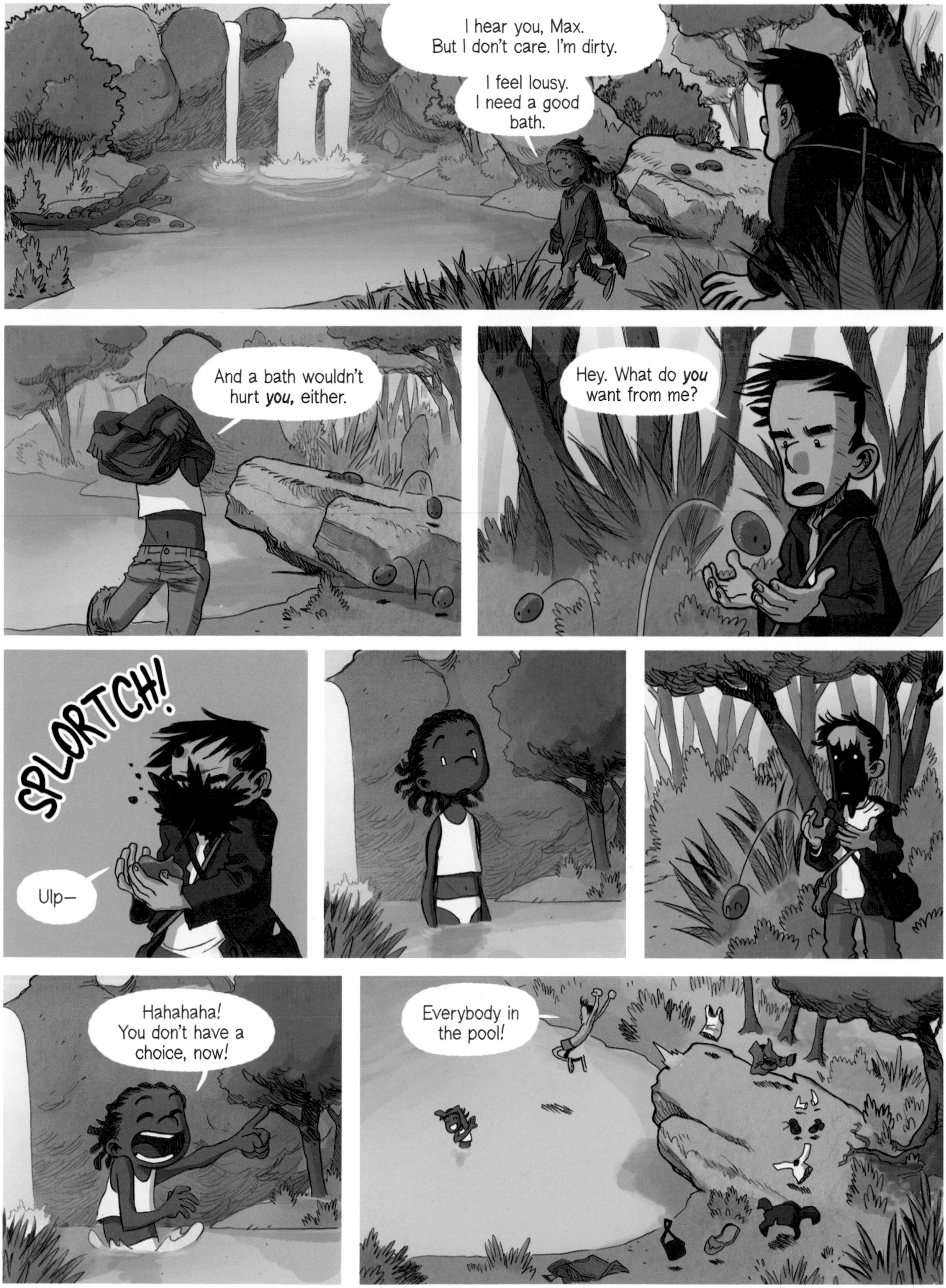

I hear you, Max.
But I don't care. I'm dirty.
I feel lousy.
I need a good bath.
And a bath wouldn't hurt *you,* either.
Hey. What do *you* want from me?
SPLORTCH!
Ulp—
Hahahaha!
You don't have a choice, now!
Everybody in the pool!

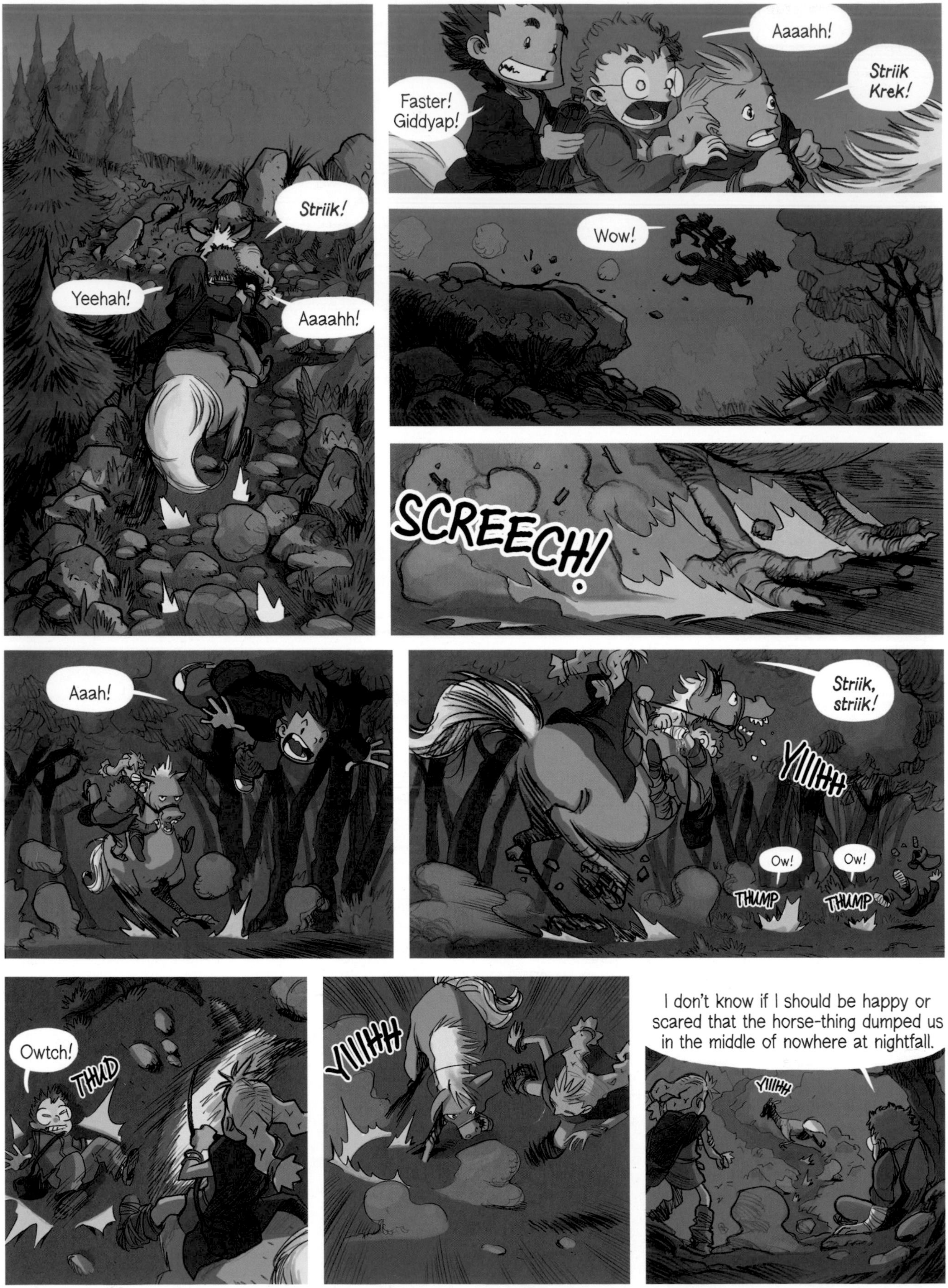
Striik!
Yeehah!
Aaaahh!
Faster! Giddyap!
Aaaahh!
Striik Krek!
Wow!
SCREECH!
Aaah!
Striik, striik!
YIIIHH
Ow!
THUMP
Ow!
THUMP
Owtch!
THUD
YIIIHH
I don't know if I should be happy or scared that the horse-thing dumped us in the middle of nowhere at nightfall.
YIIIHH

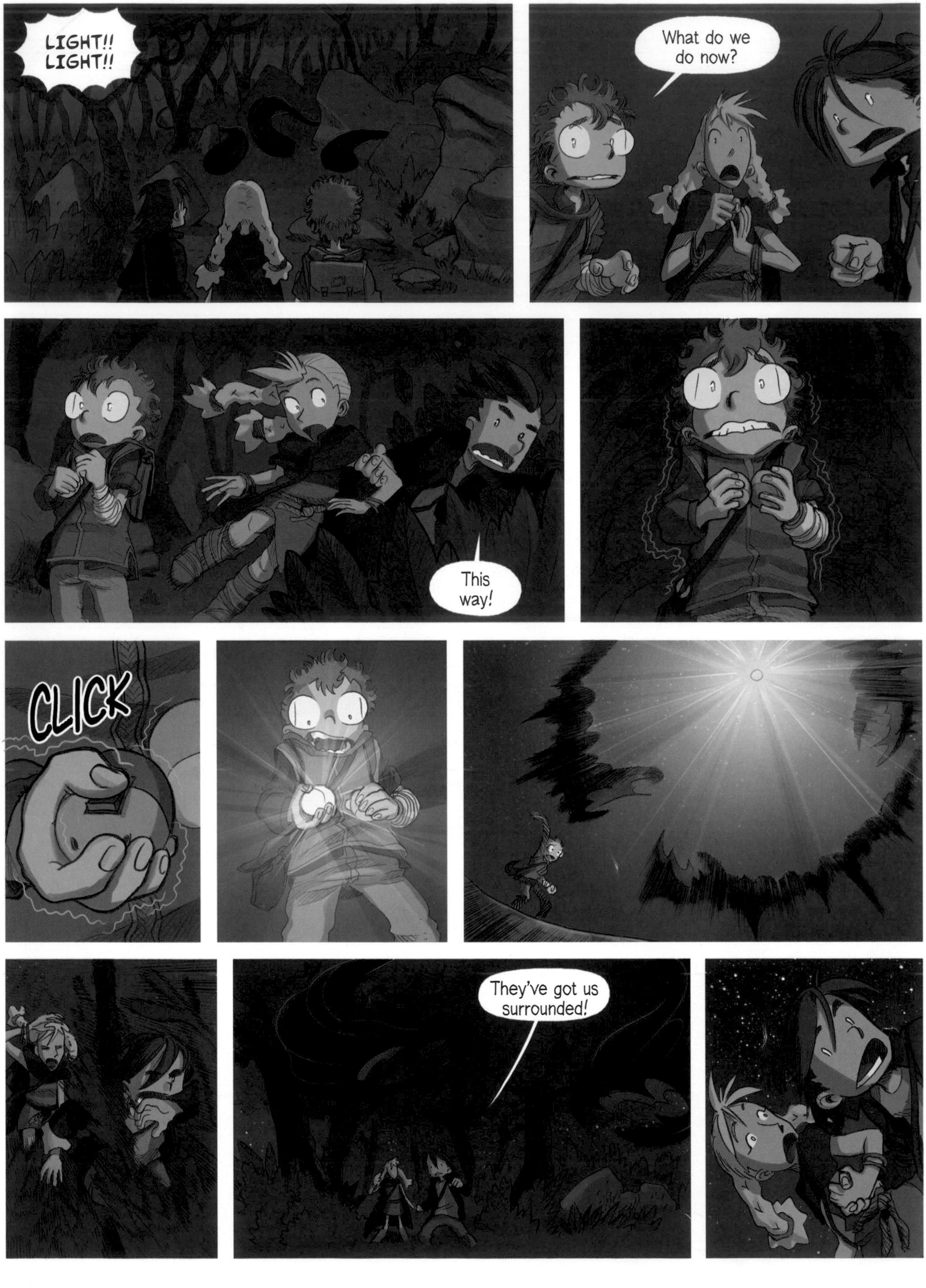
LIGHT!! LIGHT!!
What do we do now?
This way!
CLICK
They've got us surrounded!

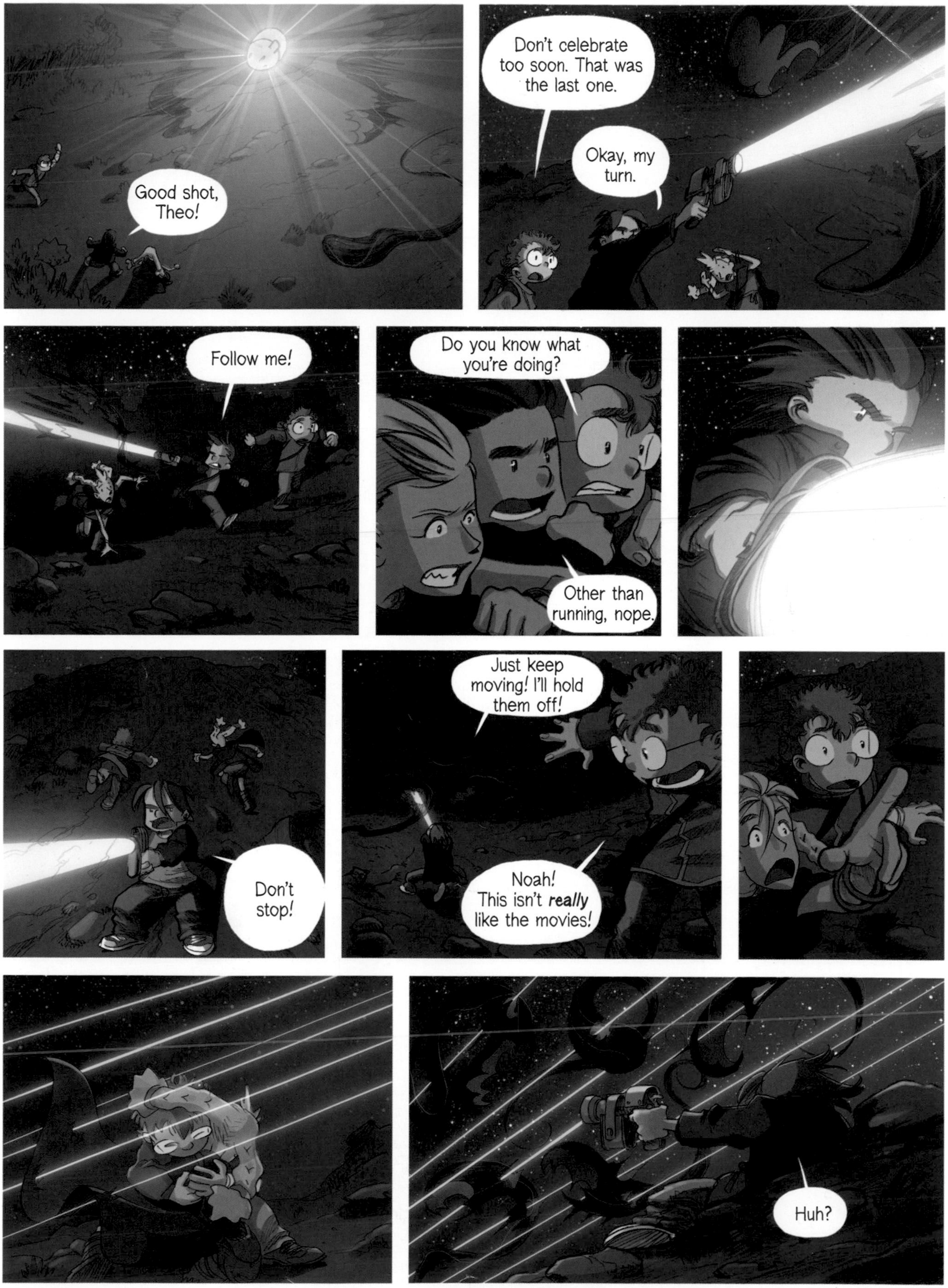
Good shot, Theo!
Don't celebrate too soon. That was the last one.
Okay, my turn.
Follow me!
Do you know what you're doing?
Other than running, nope.
Don't stop!
Just keep moving! I'll hold them off!
Noah! This isn't **really** like the movies!
Huh?

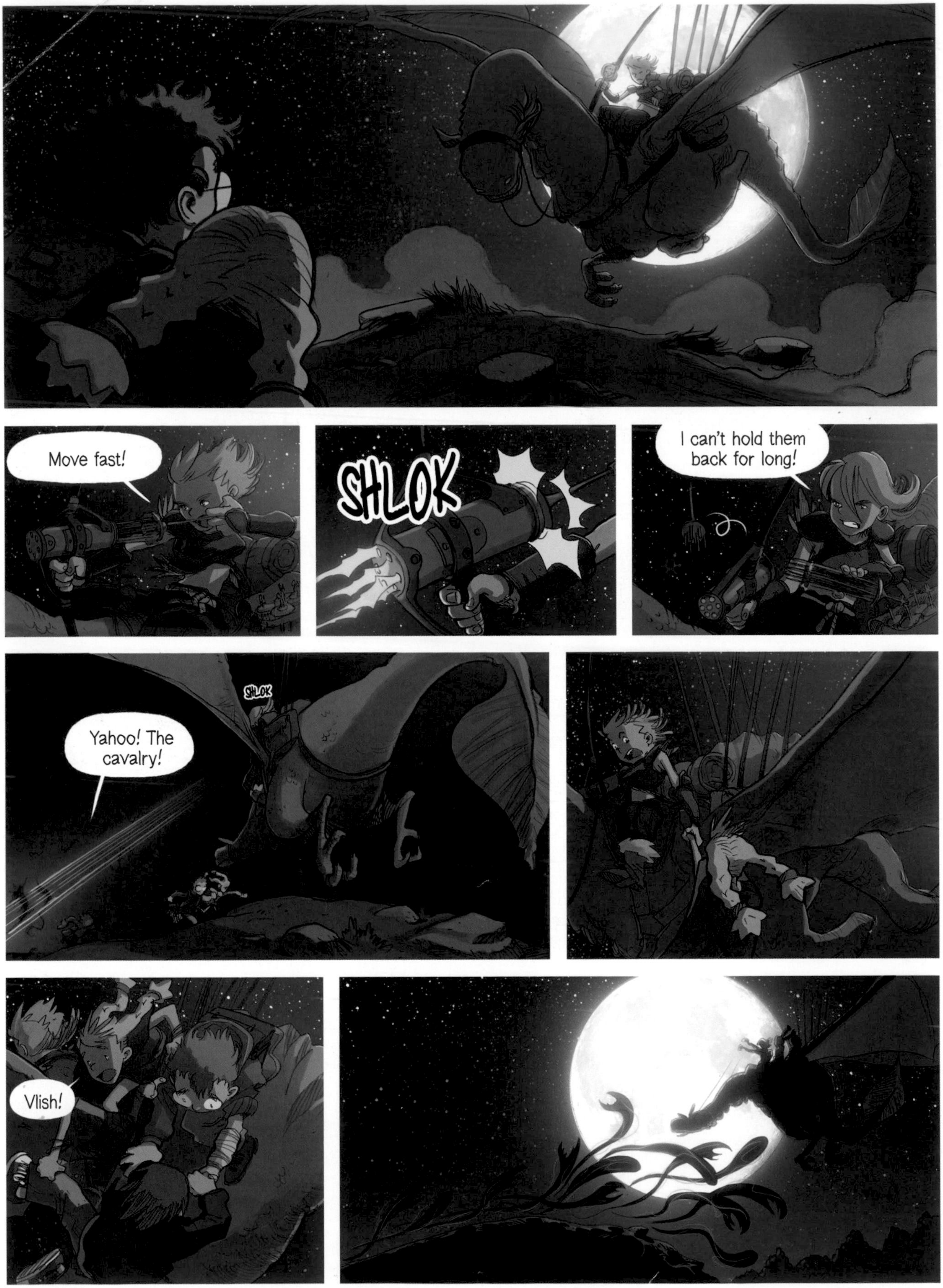

Move fast!
SHLOK
I can't hold them back for long!
SHLOK
Yahoo! The cavalry!
Vlish!

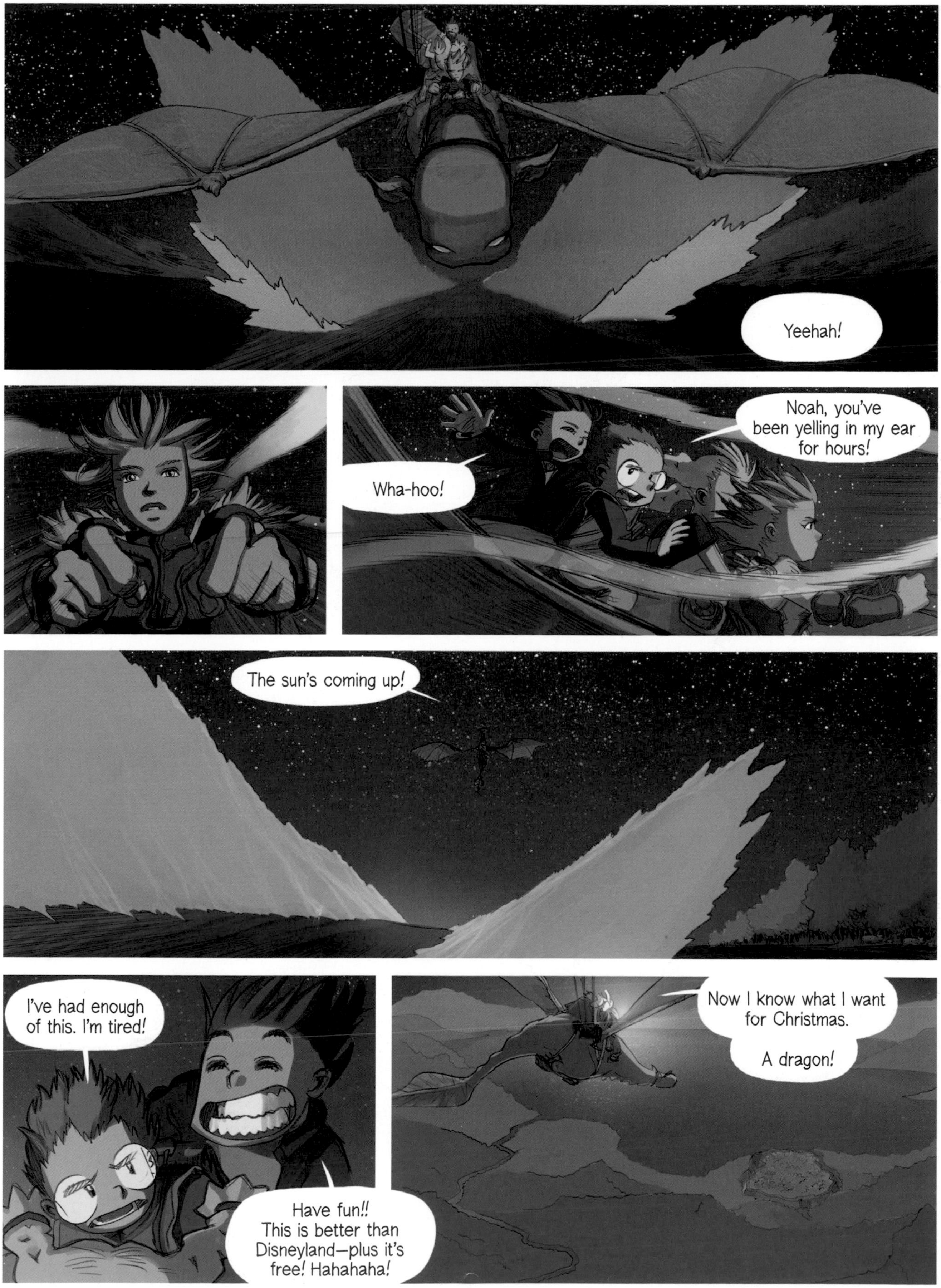
Yeehah!
Wha-hoo!
Noah, you've been yelling in my ear for hours!
The sun's coming up!
I've had enough of this. I'm tired!
Have fun!! This is better than Disneyland—plus it's free! Hahahaha!
Now I know what I want for Christmas.
A dragon!

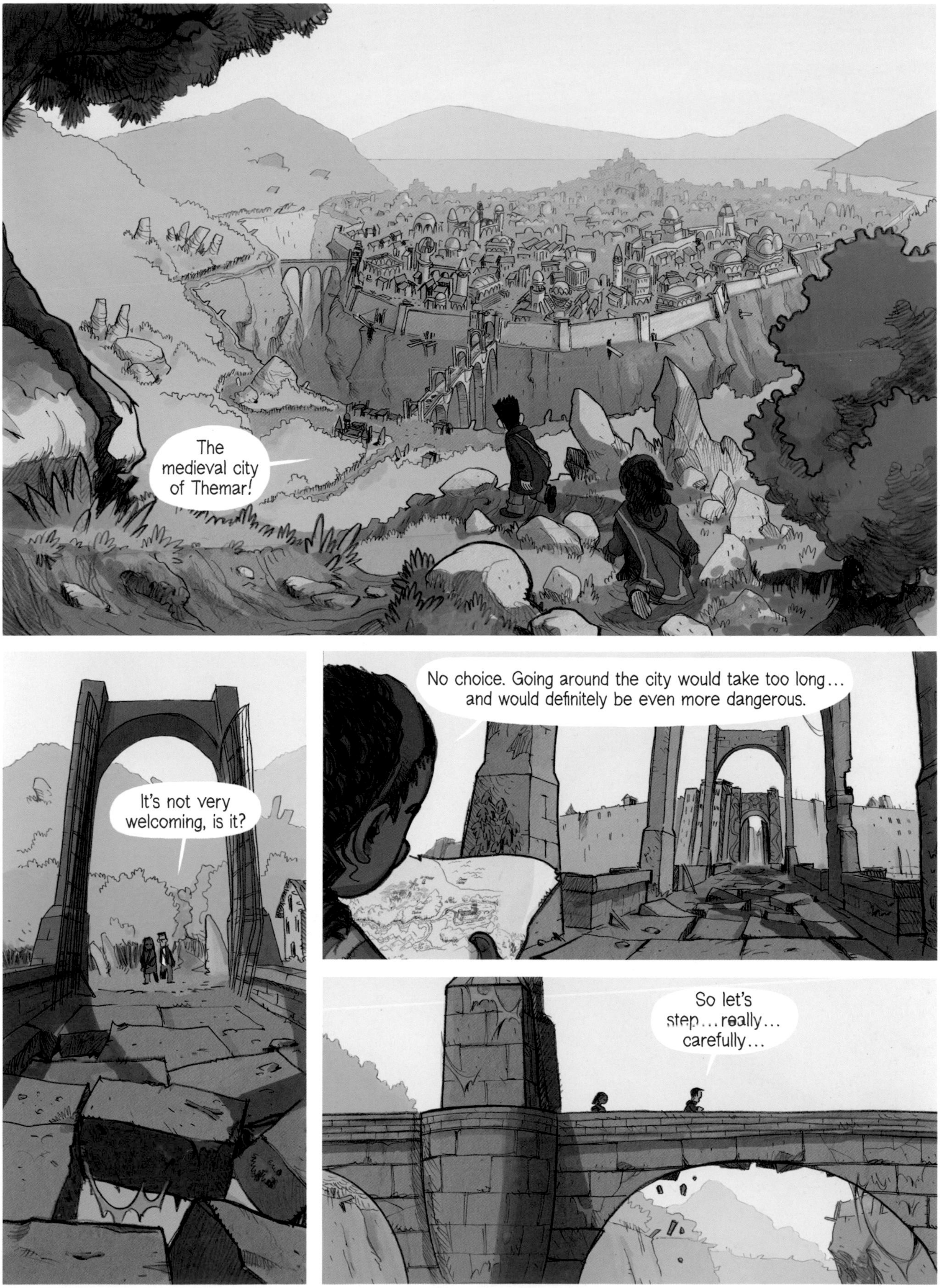
The medieval city of Themar!
It's not very welcoming, is it?
No choice. Going around the city would take too long... and would definitely be even more dangerous.
So let's step... really... carefully...

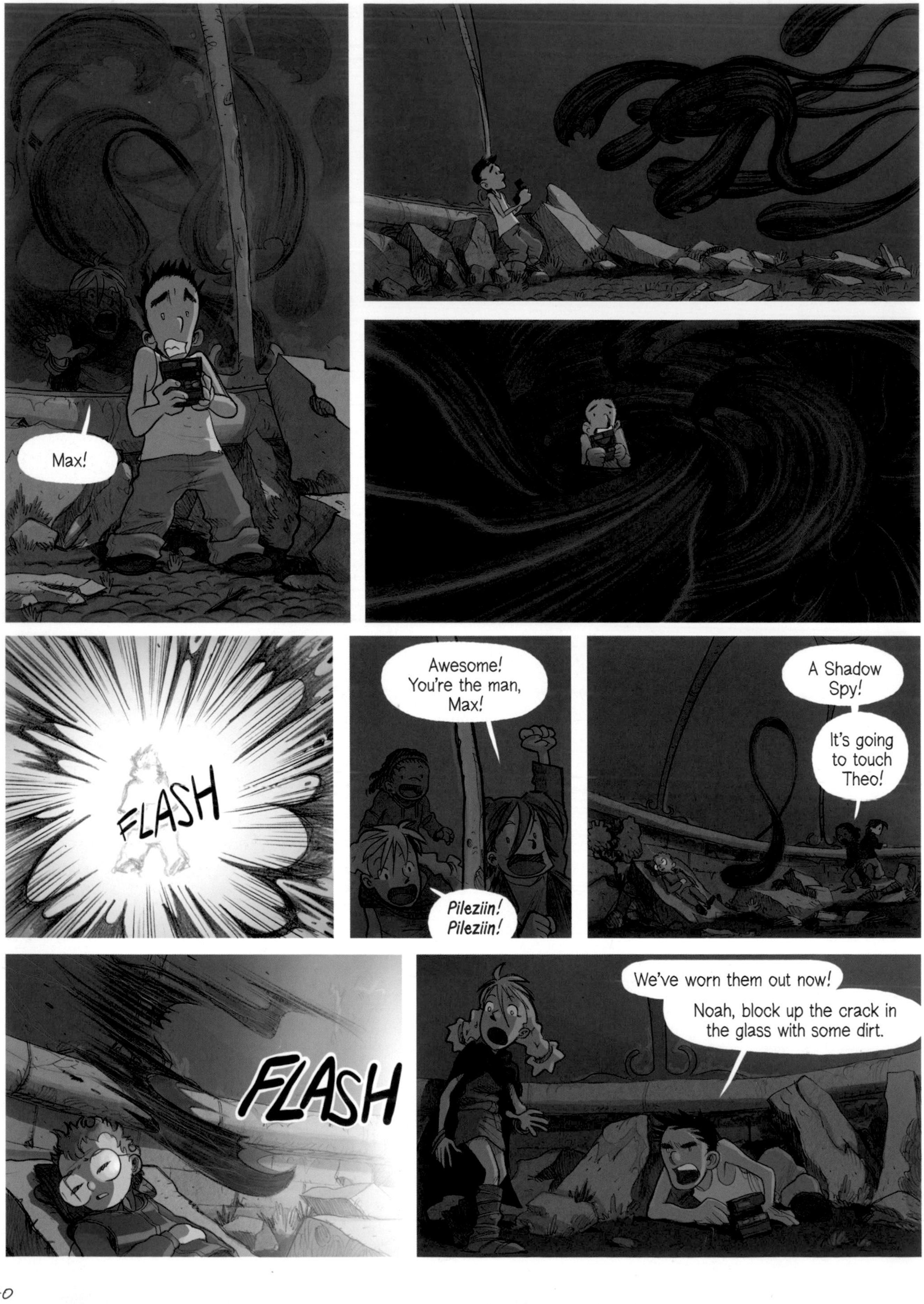

Max!
FLASH
Awesome! You're the man, Max!
Pileziin! Pileziin!
A Shadow Spy!
It's going to touch Theo!
FLASH
We've worn them out now!
Noah, block up the crack in the glass with some dirt.

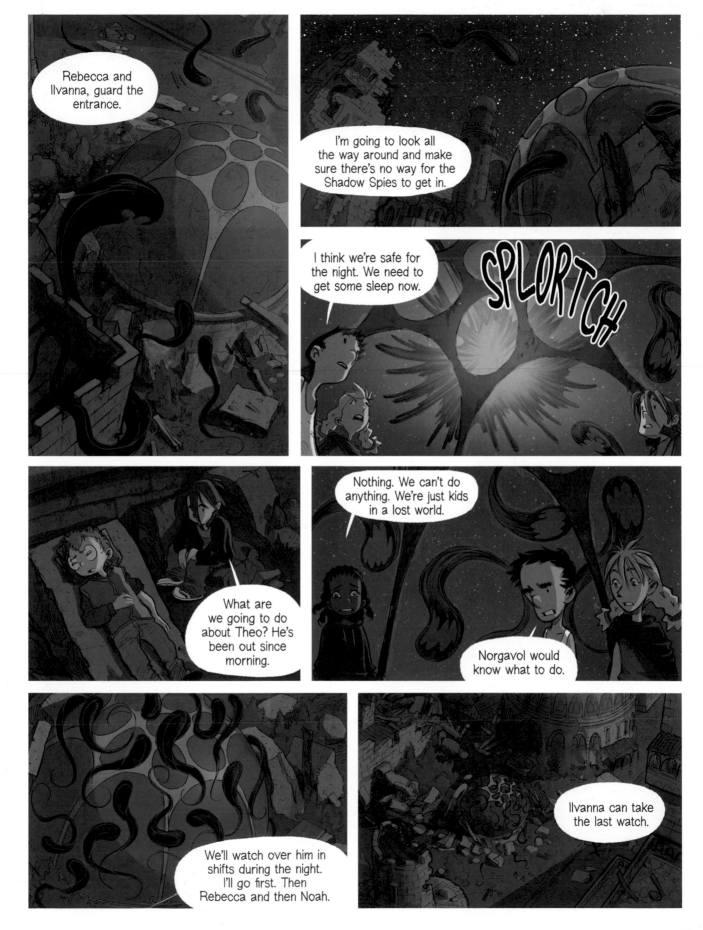

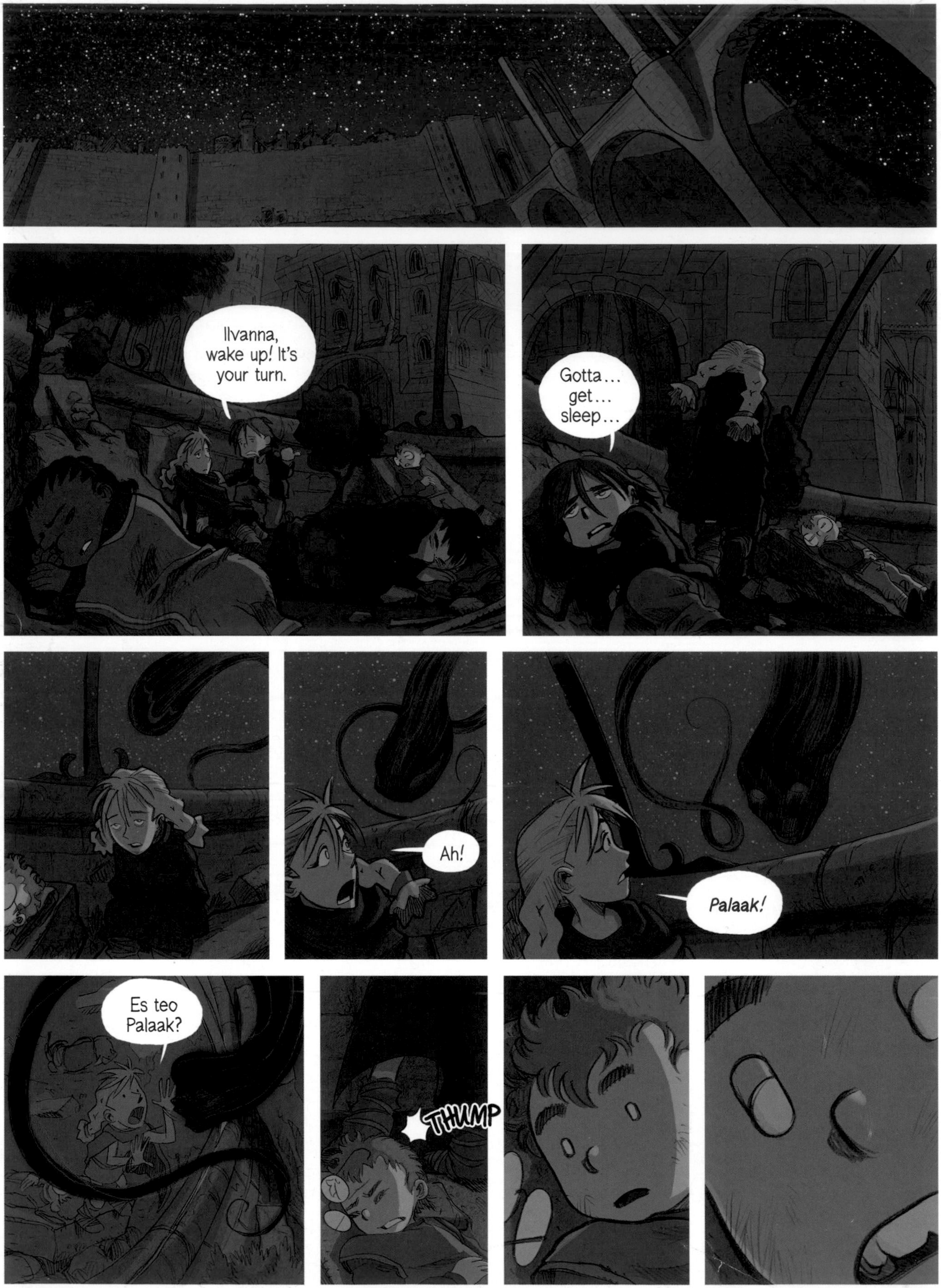
Ilvanna, wake up! It's your turn.
Gotta... get... sleep...
Ah!
Palaak!
Es teo Palaak?
THUMP

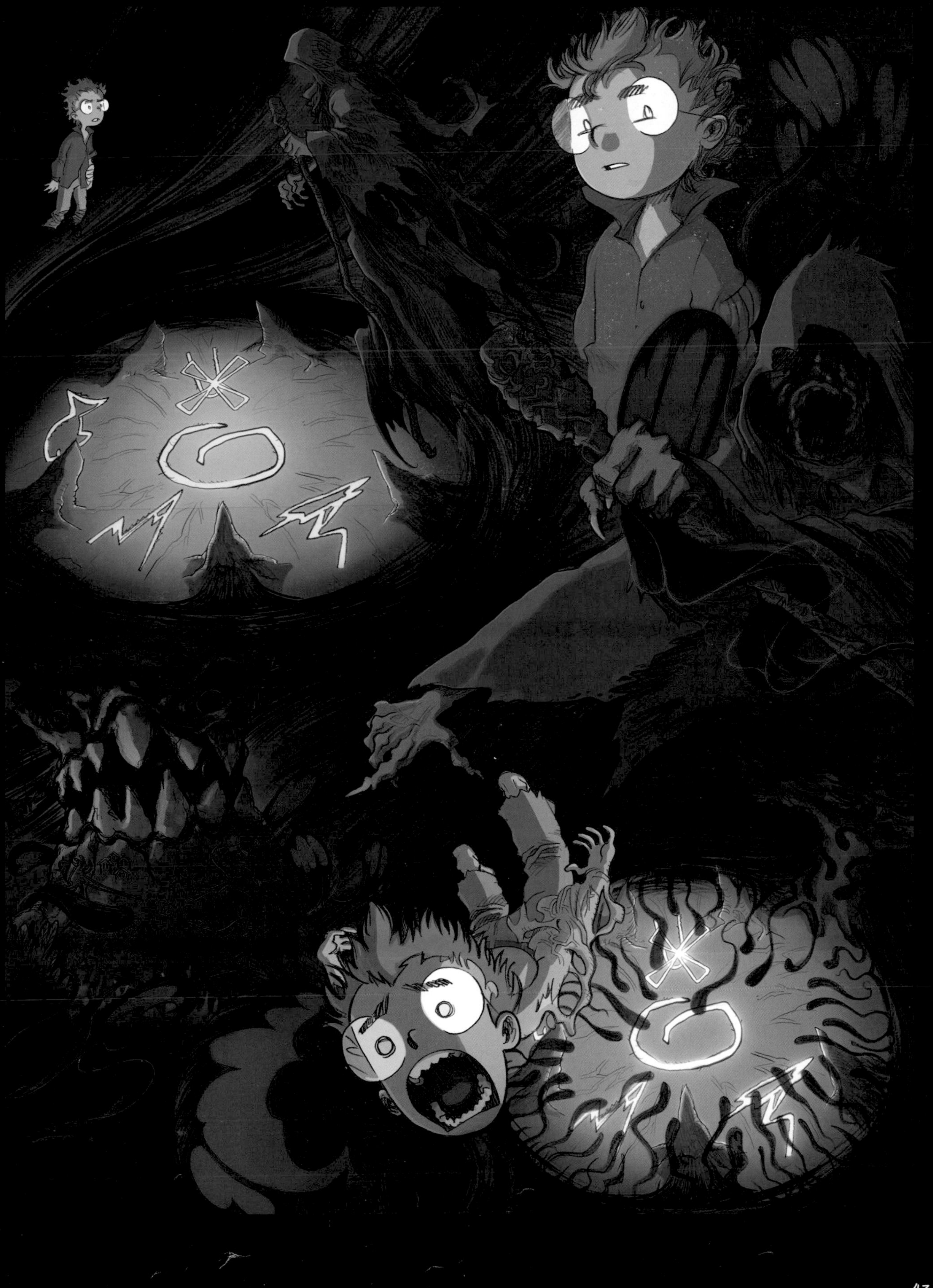

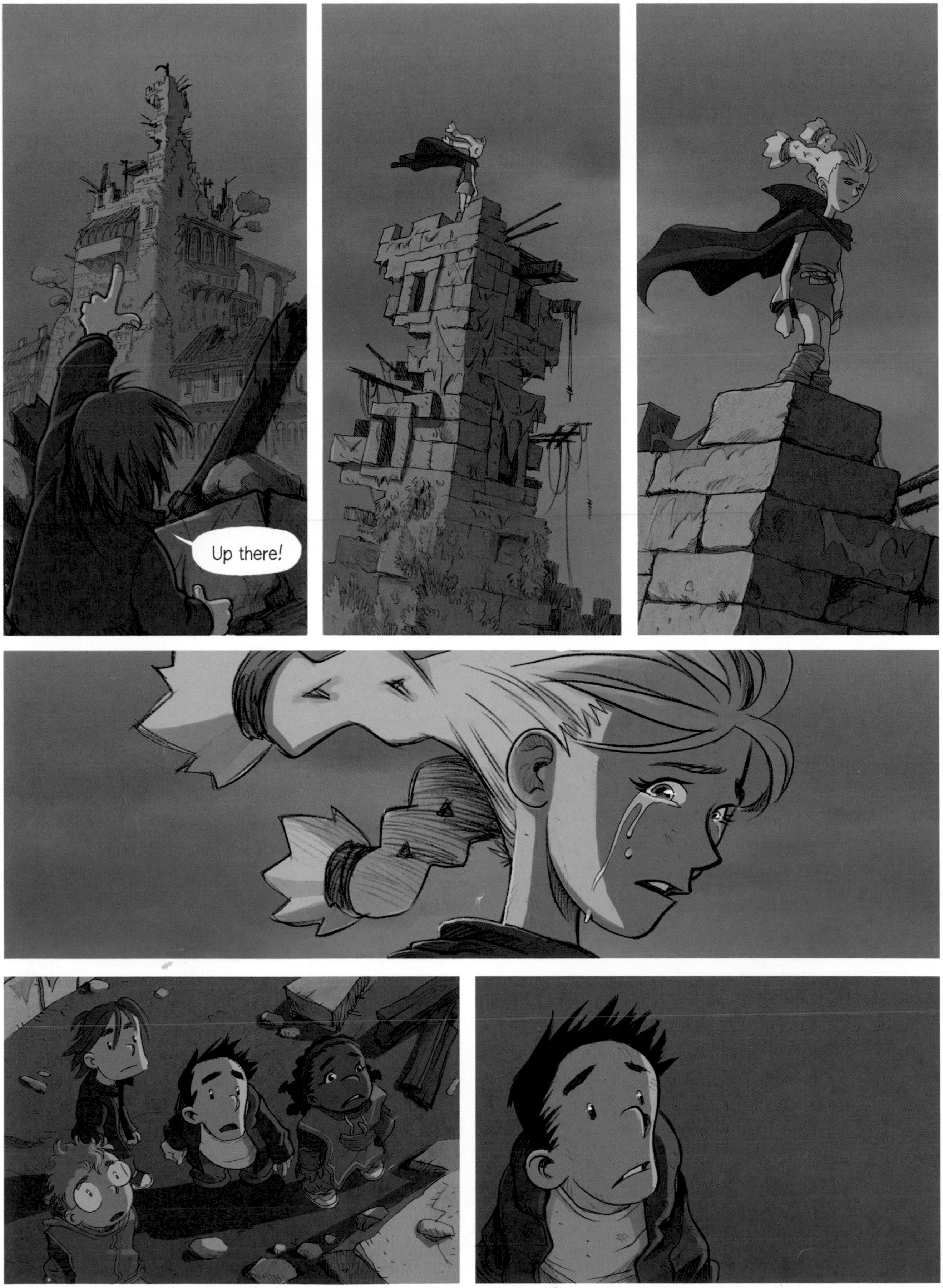
Up there!

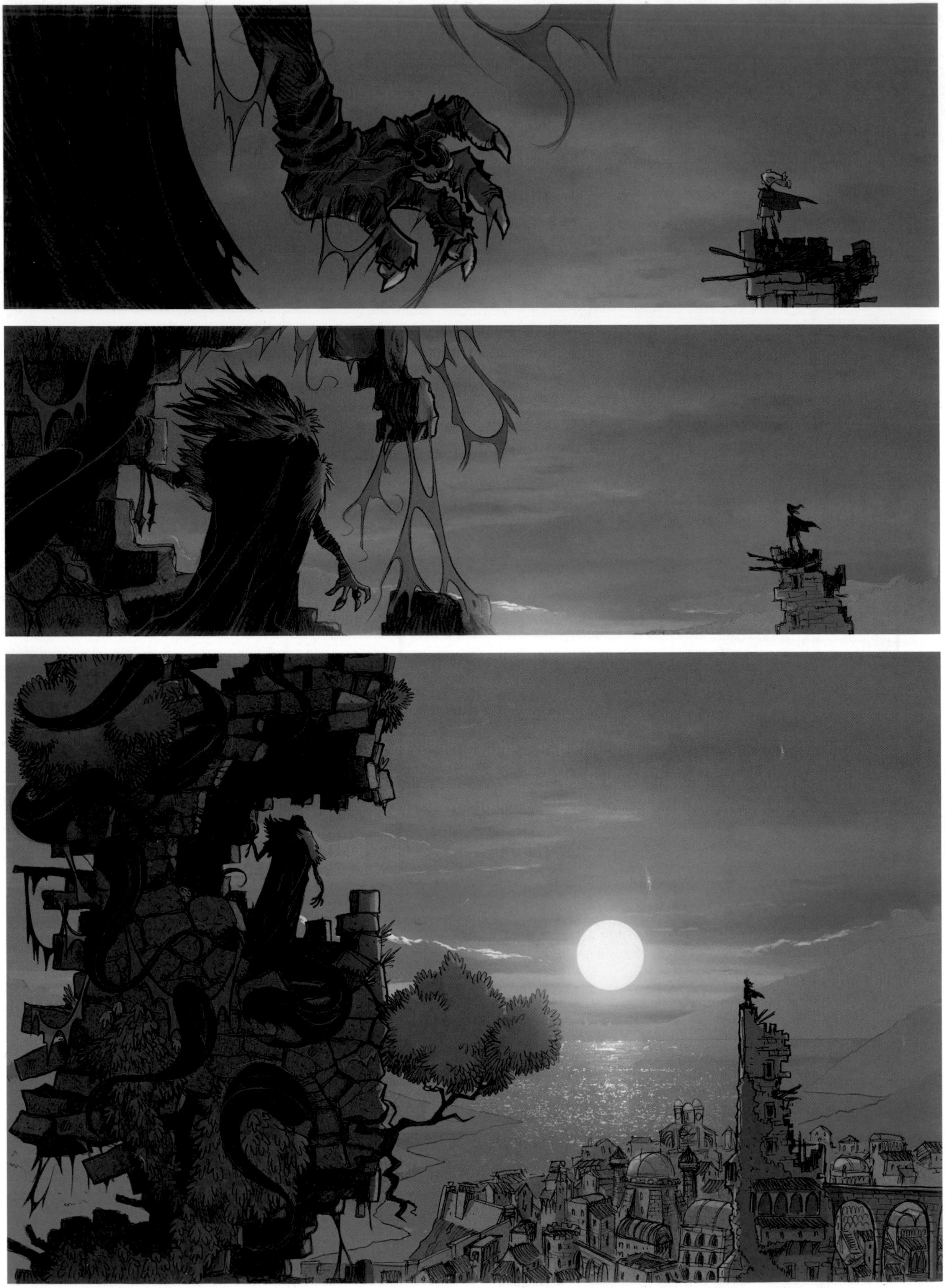

NExt Episode...

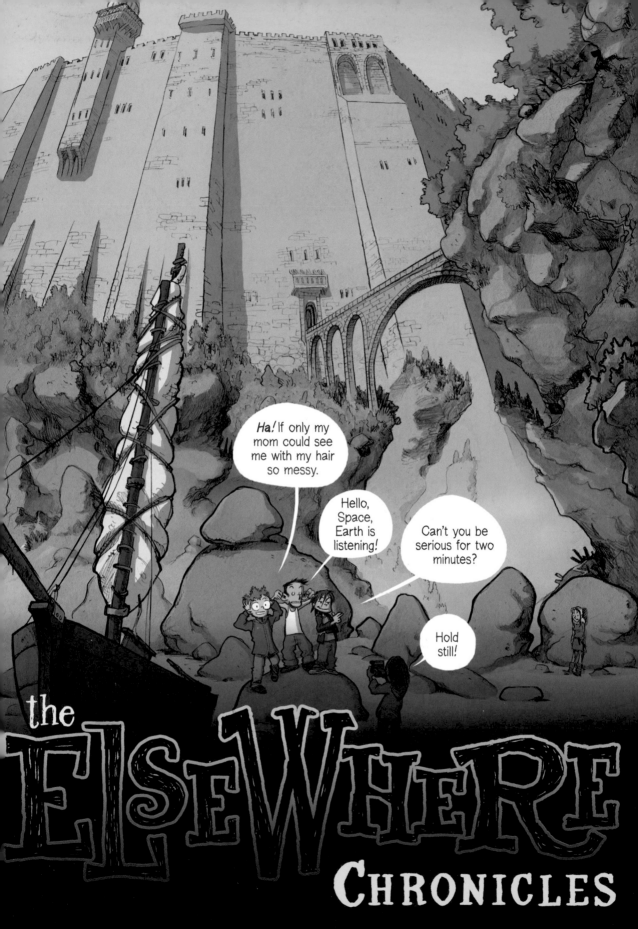

Art by Bannister
Story by Nykko
Colors by Jaffré
Translation by Carol Klio Burrell

First American edition published in 2009 by Graphic Universe™.
Published by arrangement with S.A. DUPUIS, Belgium.

Graphic Universe™
A division of Lerner Publishing Group, Inc.
241 First Avenue North
Minneapolis, MN 55401 U.S.A.

Website address: www.lernerbooks.com

Library of Congress Cataloging-in-Publication Data

Bannister.
[Ombres. English]
The Shadow Spies / art by Bannister ; story by Nykko ; [colors by Jaffré ;
translation by Carol Klio Burrell]. — 1st American ed.
p.   cm. — (The ElseWhere chronicles ; bk. 2)
Summary: Rebecca, Max, Theo, and Noah continue their journey through the other world
in search of a way home, pursued by the Shadow Spies and the mysterious Master of Shadows.
ISBN: 978-0-7613-4460-5 (lib. bdg. : alk. paper)
1. Graphic novels. [1. Graphic novels. 2. Horror stories.] I. Nykko. II. Jaffré.
III. Burrell, Carol Klio. IV. Title.
PZ7.7.B34Sm 2009
741.5'973—dc22   2008039443

Manufactured in the United States of America
1 2 3 4 5 6 - BP - 14 13 12 11 10 09

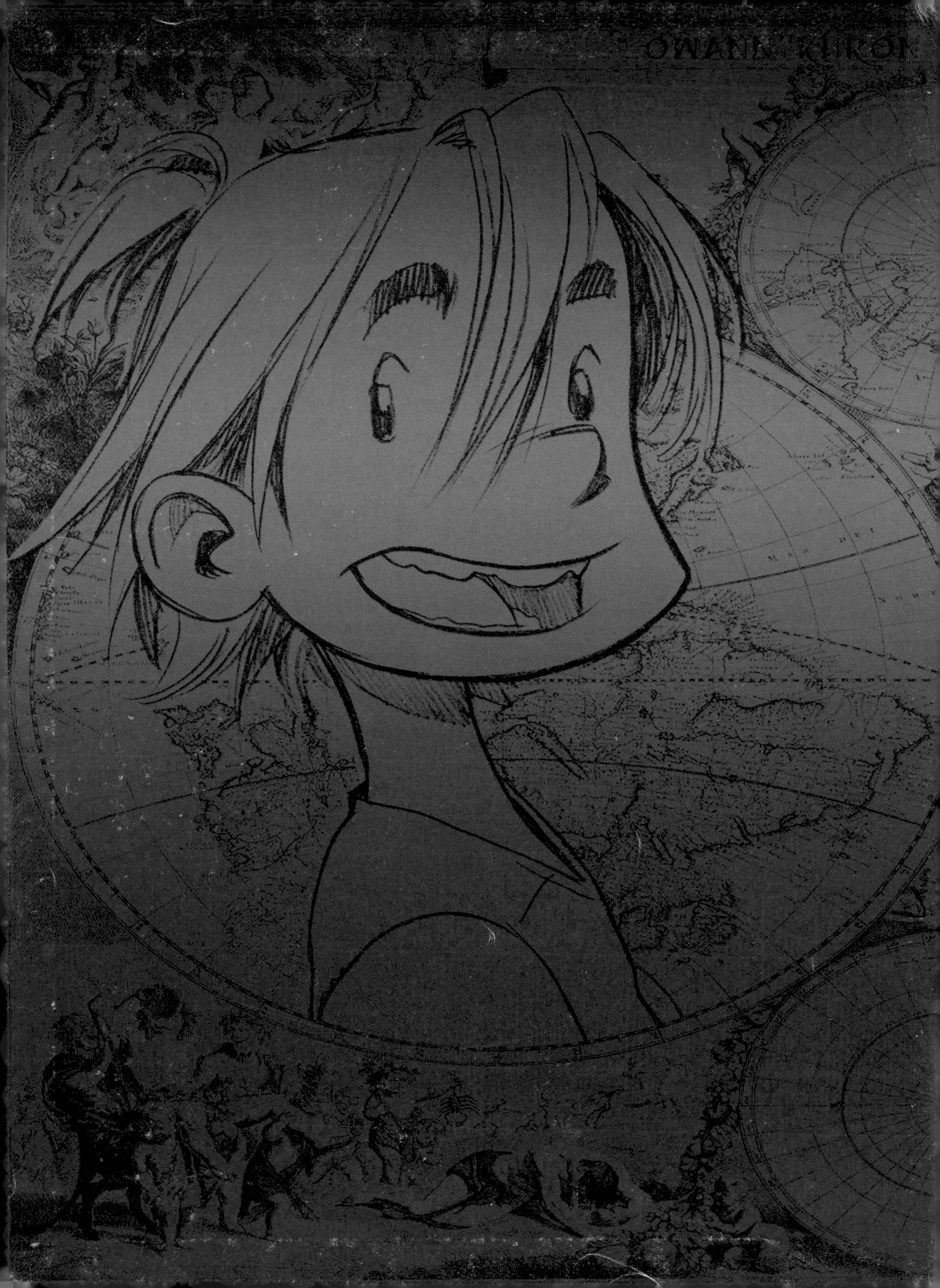